SUZANNA'S JOURNEY

SUZANNA'S JOURNEY

CINDY GREER

XULON PRESS

Xulon Press
2301 Lucien Way #415
Maitland, FL 32751
407.339.4217
www.xulonpress.com

© 2022 by Cindy Greer

All rights reserved solely by the author. The author guarantees all contents are original and do not infringe upon the legal rights of any other person or work. No part of this book may be reproduced in any form without the permission of the author.

Due to the changing nature of the Internet, if there are any web addresses, links, or URLs included in this manuscript, these may have been altered and may no longer be accessible. The views and opinions shared in this book belong solely to the author and do not necessarily reflect those of the publisher. The publisher therefore disclaims responsibility for the views or opinions expressed within the work.

Unless otherwise indicated, Scripture quotations taken from the Holy Bible, New International Version (NIV). Copyright © 1973, 1978, 1984, 2011 by Biblica, Inc.™. Used by permission. All rights reserved.

Paperback ISBN-13: 978-1-66286-631-9

Ebook ISBN-13: 978-1-66286-632-6

Contents

Dedication vii
Chapter 1 1
Chapter 2 8
Chapter 3 10
Chapter 4 13
Chapter 5 17
Chapter 6 20
Chapter 7 24
Chapter 8 28
Chapter 9 31
Chapter 10 36
Chapter 11 41
Chapter 12 43
Chapter 13 46
Chapter 14 50
Chapter 15 54
Chapter 16 57
Chapter 17 61
Chapter 18 65
Chapter 19 68
Chapter 20 72
Chapter 21 76
Chapter 22 79
Chapter 23 81
Chapter 24 82
Chapter 25 86
Chapter 26 88
Chapter 27 91
Chapter 28 94
Chapter 29 96
Chapter 30 99
Chapter 31 102
Chapter 32 105
Chapter 33 108
Chapter 34 111
Chapter 36 114
Chapter 37 118
Chapter 38 121
Chapter 39 125
Chapter 40 127
Chapter 41 132
Chapter 42 135
Chapter 43 138
Chapter 44 145

DEDICATION

I want to dedicate this work to my one and only, my soulmate, but most of all the love of my life. After fifty-one years, our lives only get more interesting, challenging, and blessed. Our love has only grown with our amazing family. You are the biggest supporter of my dreams. You have allowed me, encouraged me, provided for me, and helped me grow into who I am today. You encouraged me to follow my dreams. You always have been the answer to a young eight-year-old girl's prayer. Thank you, Bud Greer, my Prince Charming.

To my Lord and Savior, thank you for the passion you planted in my heart to pursue, grow, and give me the courage to never give up or give in, and to live a life of gratitude to the King of Kings who saved my life more than once. To my pastors, Jeff and Dina Hackert, my growth as a Christian came from your encouragement and your belief that with God all things are possible and to keep on keeping on.

Finally a special thank you to Jackie Claycomb for her time and encouragement. Her proofreading skills helped me catch many mistakes before advancing forward and her encouragement gave me the boldness to follow my dreams.

CHAPTER 1

It was a cold, blustery day when Suzanna stepped outside from her Marriot Hotel room to travel the thirty miles or so left of her journey. She would have rather completed her trip the night before, but the weather did not want to cooperate. She was tired from the eight hours she had already driven. Besides, she thought it best to not show up unexpected so late in the evening. There was a small dusting of snow on the roads that twirled from the breeze of the traffic, which was already more than she expected in rural Iowa. The weather didn't want to cooperate with anyone. The unusually bitter cold didn't typically come this early in the year. It should still be fall weather in late September with rain and a chill, not snow and bitter cold. She wondered if that meant they were going to see a harsh early winter or was it just a warning of what was to come next month. Their winter came sooner than hers did in rural Kentucky. She already missed home. It was raining and chilly, but that was easier tolerated than this. As she crossed the bridge in Council Bluffs into Omaha, Nebraska she began to get a little nervous reconnecting with cousins she hadn't seen nor spoken to in twenty years. She was too afraid they would not receive her visit well. The GPS led her to an exquisite neighborhood and her destination was the next street over in a place called West Highland Cove. "Well, here I am," she thought. It was around 11:30 on a Saturday morning as she pulled into the long driveway that circled in front of the house. Nothing like announcing "here I am guys," before she even introduced herself. Someone opened the front door before she got out of the car, a comfortable ride all in all. She had purchased the Nissen Pathfinder specifically for this trip.

Suzana stepped out of the car, carrying only her cheap black and white plaid purse she got on sale at Borders and walked up several steps before a shaggy, black-haired teenage boy wearing only red boxer shorts and a white t-shirt asked her, "Yeah, do you need to see Mom or Dad?"

"Mom, I think," Suzanna replied.

"Oh OK, just a minute." He slammed the door shut in her face.

It only took a moment or two even though it felt like eternity before a middle aged, shoulder length dark-haired woman opened the door and casually asked me what I needed.

"Are you Donna Williams?" I asked.

"Who wants to know," she answered.

"Well, if you are Donna, then, I am your cousin Suzanna from Kentucky."

She opened the door wider and stood back to let her in. "My goodness Suzanna, it has been a long time. We haven't heard anything from your side of the family since our parents died." She replied with a warmth to her voice. "Your Mom and my mom both died shortly apart from each other. Come on in. Are you up here on vacation with family?"

"No," Suzanna nervously replied. "I came up on my own. My sister, Debra, wanted to come with me, but I needed to do this on my own. Plus, it was important to make the trip as soon as I could."

"Come into the family room," Donna said. "The kids are playing video games on the big TV," she said as she welcomed Suzanna into her home. "There is a fireplace in the family room where you can get warmed up. I'll grab us cups of hot chocolate. Marshmallows or without?" She asked.

"With. I love marshmallows." She replied, "Thank you, it is bitterly cold outside today." Suzanna looked around. "Are all the children yours?" She noticed four boys and one girl glued to the biggest television built into the wall that she had ever seen. It was impressive to say the least, she thought to herself.

"Oh, no," she answered with a chuckle as she walked from the large open kitchen into the family room where Suzanna sat on a large mahogany reclining chair that faced the big, warm fireplace built with the traditional red brick and large beautiful mantel full of pictures of memories. "The three boys are neighborhood friends from next door. Mike is the one who answered the door. He was named after my brother Mike. The older and more mature one, the girl, is Abigail. She lives down the street and all the boys hope she picks one of them to go with her to the Thanksgiving Dance they have at school the week before Thanksgiving. Mike is our late in life surprise. The two little ones, the boy and girl, are twins and belong to Samantha. She had to work overnight and won't be home for a couple more hours. She is a nurse at Omaha's General Hospital. She and her husband just recently went through a very contentious divorce, so I am helping her out tonight because her babysitter was sick.

"You all had all girls, didn't you?" Suzanna asked.

Laughing, Donna replied, "Yes, we did. That makes Mike a blessing and surprise wrapped into one special bundle. They are upstairs taking a nap. "Donna was always the prettiest cousin," Suzanna thought. She usually kept her thick, dark black hair at just a little past shoulder length. Her dark complexion looked like her dad's. Suzanna thought about her Uncle Dave. He was half Apache Indian. He was always warm and caring and had a witty sense of humor. Donna was much like that. She remembered living with them for six months in California while her dad was looking for work. When he found a job in a tuna factory, Suzanna's family moved into their own home. It had felt nice to have her own bedroom and all, but she really missed her cousins. They were able to do more things together the summer they lived with them. Especially after school events which was every Tuesday and Thursday through the summer. They had many arts and crafts and some sports. After living in California for two years, her parents decided to move to Kentucky where her dad was born. They bought a small farm in the country. Daddy promised her a horse of her own. She had to share with her sister, Debra, but it wasn't so bad because Deb didn't have much interest in horses. She loved the cats around the farm. Suzanna's daddy took them out on trail rides with him. Best part of Kentucky was seen on the back of the old mare Ginger he bought her thinking back on those special family times. She remembered the English Spaniel puppy his Aunt Willow gave her, which became Suzanna's constant companion when they first moved to Kentucky. Maybe being such a huge animal lover helped her get over missing her cousins and family from both Omaha and San Diego.

Suzanna began to feel it was time to tell her purpose for coming all this way alone. "Donna, I had a reason for coming to see you. It is hard for me to bring it up, so I am just going to spit it out."

"Of course, Suzanna," Donna answered softly. She suspected something was bothering her cousin or she wouldn't come this far after all these years for no good reason and all alone. They both had finished their hot chocolate and Suzanna thanked her as she put her cup down on the coffee table beside her chair. She pulled the mysterious paperwork from her large purse before she began to tell her story.

She laughed a nervous laugh before going any further and clasped her hands together in her lap on top of the paperwork.

"Well, my brother found some papers in my mother's things," Suzanna said. "She stayed with them after her cancer got really bad. When she died, they boxed all her things up and never went through any of it because it was too painful. Recently, they decided to sort through them to make more space for a much-needed sewing room. They thought they would sort through everything. Anything of value they brought to me to decide if it was something Debra or I wanted. What they found astonished them, and they immediately came to see me."

"My goodness. It doesn't have to do with your mom's dad does it?" she asked.

"Well, yes. What made you guess that?" Suzanna looked at her quizzically as she looked back.

"My mother, told me a story once that, Aunt Jeannie's father, was quite rich and left all he had to his only daughter, but we never heard any more about it after Jason Burns died. He was who your grandmother was married to when she died. Your mother hated him so much He never told her about the inheritance and Mom never mentioned it because she figured he was just rambling about something he knew nothing about. He lied about so

Chapter 1

many things. Mom just took it with a grain of salt. We figured if it was true, you all would surely know. Why are you coming to me?"

"I didn't know who else I could turn to up here," Suzanna said. "So many years have passed by and none of us are getting any younger. So let me explain my problem and see if you have any fresh insight. Lawrence and Diana came to my house three days ago with these papers from a lawyer up here and I didn't know if you had heard of him." Suzanna picked up the manilla envelop from her lap and with shaky hands held it out to Donna to read.

Donna held out her hand as Suzanna pulled out the paperwork. She gasped as she read the beginning paragraph, looked up at her curiously before reading on until she read the complete document. "Oh my, how are we going to deal with this?"

Suzanna was thankful she said "we" because it meant she was going to help—she hoped.

"I don't know, I was hoping you had some ideas as to where to start."

"I think the beginning should be looking up the lawyer who wrote up these documents. I have heard his name. He is retired and has two sons who have taken over the practice." Donna sounded a bit hesitant but also a bit hopeful.

"So, are you hopeful they will help or are you a little anxious to turn to them for help?" Suzanna asked her quietly, hoping for a positive response.

Donna was quiet for a minute, which caused Suzanna's anxiety level to skyrocket.

"One of his sons is an arrogant, selfish man who doesn't do anything to help anyone unless it can line his own pockets with gold," Donna said. "I hear you can't ask for one or the other. Who you get is a luck of the draw. That's how they run their father's practice."

"Maybe we could go speak to their father, especially since he drew up the papers," Suzanna offered.

"That would be nice except he died from COVID-19 last year." She handed Suzanna back her paperwork before stating the obvious. "That's a lot of money. And that practice would love some of it."

"I thought the same," Suzanna answered.

"I do know one thing for sure," Donna said as she looked into Suzanna's desperate eyes hoping that what she was about to say was obvious and not come as a big shock to her, "there is little we can do until Monday morning and when we walk into the lawyer's office, we need to be prepared for anything. Good, bad, or ugly."

Suzanna nodded affirmatively and said, "Agreed."

"So, do you attend church?" Donna asked.

Suzanna nodded in the affirmative again.

"We belong to a Christian Church just around the corner. It has a big congregation with around a thousand members. If you would like, you can stay here until we get this all worked out. We have a nice spare bedroom at the top of the stairs. You are more than welcome to come to church with us, but there's no pressure if you'd prefer to sleep in and get some rest tomorrow. You probably want to settle in a bit now so let me help you get your things. You are more than welcome to join us in the morning but don't feel obligated."

All Suzanna could do was smile and thank Donna for her help and hospitality, and she would love to go with them to church in the morning. Suzanna was tired and the bedroom was welcoming, and the bed was so snuggly and soft with four big pillows to sink into and a rosy coral bedspread and matching quilt. It didn't take her but a minute to close her eyes and she was out until she heard a faint knock on the door. When she opened her eyes and stretched her arms, she noticed it was already dark. She spoke only two words, "come in" before Donna poked her head in and offered for Suzanna to join them for dinner. Suzanna was hungry, so of course she accepted the offer.

"Let me call my sister and let her know I am here and doing okay and then I will be right down," Suzanna said.

Donna's son and husband were just like her, full of jolly and good humor, teasing one another and her husband was sweet and gracious. Anything she needed, he said he would try and get it, but Suzanna told him she was fine. After dinner and a little small talk, Suzanna settled back into her bedroom, curled up under the covers, and turned the television on low volume. It had

Chapter 1

been a long while since she had listened to Omaha news. Donna poked her head in to tell her she would let her know when to get up for church.

"You have your own private bathroom in here," Donna said. "I didn't know if you knew it or not."

"Actually, I have been so dead tired, all I have done is jump in bed," Suzanna replied.

She chuckled with her. "Good night then, sleep well."

"Thanks, I'm sure I will."

Chapter 2

Sunday was relaxing. The church was packed, and she felt blessed by the worship and the message. Donna's family introduced Suzanna to the pastor, Steven Landry. He was warm and friendly, and she enjoyed his pleasant and polite conversation. Donna invited him to eat lunch with them. At first, he wasn't receptive, but eventually he agreed. His wife died three years ago and they never had any children.

They ate at a steakhouse Suzanna didn't recognize or remember, however the food and conversation was enjoyable. It was only the four adults because the kiddos had plans with friends. Donna filled Steven in on Suzanna's dilemma and he offered to go to the lawyer's office with them on Monday. Suzanna shook her head no and before it came out of her mouth, Donna accepted his kind offer.

The following morning came too quickly. Suzanna wasn't ready when the doorbell rang, so Steven came in for a cup of hot coffee. He was even more pleasant, and his warm smile was alarmingly alluring in a way that made Suzanna feel everything was going to be fine even when she was afraid they were not going to be.

Suzanna held out her hand as she offered, "Dr. Landry, good to see you this morning."

"Just Steven, please," he said. Steven softly but firmly shook Suzanna's hand with a quirky grin.

"Of course, Just Steven," Suzanna replied and wondered if she was blushing before realizing they were still holding hands. She quickly dropped

Chapter 2

his hand and turned to see Donna smiling at them before she handed him a cup of coffee and cleared her throat softly before offering him a seat around the elegant cherry red dining room table. She brought Suzanna a cup of hot chocolate with marshmallows after remembering she didn't drink coffee. We did some strategizing, and it was agreed that Donna's husband, Richard, and Steven would do most of the talking. Steven was familiar with the law firm and their lack of respect toward females.

They all rode in Donna's Suburban in silence, except for a few pleasantries. Richard drove and Donna sat in front while Steven and Suzanna rode in the two bucket seats.

"Don't be so stressed about this Suzanna," Donna coaxed. "You can't show signs of weakness or be too overconfident."

"I am not sure how to appear—catatonic maybe," Suzanna quipped back before apologizing for sounding rude.

"You didn't Suzie Q," Steven comforted her, and gave her a new nickname as well.

"Suzie Q? It fits," Donna said. She laughed as she and Richard glanced at each other, both wondering if a new romance could be blooming for their lonely pastor.

"Just relax, tthe worse part will be all over soon."

"Well, everyone put your poker faces on," Richard announced, "We're here."

Steven offered up a prayer before they all exited the Suburban and went to open Suzie Q's door.

"Thank you," Suzanna offered as he reached out his hand to help her out of the car, "for everything."

Chapter 3

The law firm was on the third floor of a beautiful, downtown office building. The whole third floor and it was a bustle of activity this Monday morning in September. As they entered the office, there was a comfortable waiting area that had the appearance of nothing Suzanna had ever seen before—dark leather seats with a coffee and donut station that invited you to help yourself. Three separate seating arrangements with three to four high-back, rich mahogany leather chairs and a round coffee table in the center. Then there was a small area that appeared to be straight to business after being greeted by the receptionist who showed you where to sit. The extra comfy or straight to business area. The receptionist's desk was hidden behind tall plants to give everyone the appearance of privacy. "Nice," she thought, but it smelled of money and she wondered how much of hers they were going to seek. They didn't have to introduce themselves. They were already expecting them. Richard called in a couple of favors from a friend to get the appointment.

Cynthia, the receptionist, showed us to the not straight to business seating area and told us Douglas Nightingale was running late and to help ourselves to some coffee and pastries. So, for an hour they sat and waited.

There was a separate, private side door and in walked a man people respected. Very well and smartly dressed in an expensive suit and tie and black genuine Italian slippers.

He smiled at Cynthia as she handed him a file, then he walked down the hall. Cynthia got up from her seat and with a genuine smile of sincerity

Chapter 3

came over and apologized for our long wait. Mondays are always very busy. Mr. Nightingale with be with us shortly. He had to make a quick phone call and he can then see us.

Twenty minutes later she came back to let us know he could see us. Richard, with his right arm across Donna's back, escorted her to a chair around an oval conference table. Steven did the same with Suzanna. It was actually comforting for her.

"Richard how are you and the family doing?" Mr. Nightingale asked in a baritone voice that had to have carried throughout the whole office building.

"Fine, just fine sir. How' bout yours? Have you and your family managed to avoid COVID-19?"

"For the most part. Both my wife and I got it in the beginning but had a mild case.   Now what can I do for you fine folks? Dr. Landry, good to see you again. Been meaning to get over there and visit your church again, but you know how it is. We just got back from the Jamaica last week. The wife, Althea, wants to go back. Not that I have any objections. We had a relaxing time now that the twins are older and do their own thing. We usually always eat at least one meal at the dining room table together." Mr. Nightingale smiled and turned his chair toward Suzanna. "Looks like we might have a little problem, Miss Suzanna. People around here consider their burial plot holy ground, not to be disturbed for any reason. However, because it isn't the grave burial spot but the headstone that needs to be lifted and the metal box removed, and the headstone will be immediately lowered and put back in place. I have already got us a preliminary hearing bright and early in the morning. I've also discussed it with Judge Walter, and he doesn't feel there will be any problem going forward. But we will know more tomorrow."

Mr. Nightingale stood, shook everyone's hand, and showed us to the door. "Nice to meet all of you. Don't worry young lady, we will get all this worked out. You guys have a pleasant day and I'll see you in the morning. Cynthia will come and show you all out, and Suzanna you will need to sign a couple of documents to make this official."

Off he went, bounding down the hall to fetch Cynthia to dismiss us. Suzanna felt like she was back in the first grade but all in all she really liked him. Let's hope first impression holds.

Chapter 4

After they left the lawyers office, they stopped at Waffle House for a bite of breakfast, early lunch. Personal preferences. Richard said they were lucky they were able to see Douglas Nightingale and not Donovan. Donovan was known to be greedy and a bit ruthless—even toward his own clients.

"Hey, Suzy Q, what's wrong?" Steven asked as he looked into her eyes."

"It's nothing," she softly answered.

He looked more intently and cupped her chin with his hand and raised her eyes to look directly into his. He had the most beautiful dark blue eyes, she noticed. "I'm sorry I don't mean to be unappreciative, but I worry this may take a very long time." She looked back at him as he let her chin down.

"You have nothing to apologize for," He offered.

"No, you don't," chimed in Donna and Richard.

"But I have already taken up so much of your time, all of you," Suzanna said.

"Woah," Donna shot back. "We all, you included, knew this may take a bit of time. And I think I can speak for all of us that we are here for you for the long haul, however long it takes. So, what's this really about?"

"I don't know, maybe I am just worried."

"I have it on good authority that this will all work out just fine," Steven spoke up.

Suzanna let out a laugh that mixed with a couple of tears that fell down her check.

"It's just, I came unexpectantly to your doorstep and all of you have been great. I really feel so at home here. It is like the last years of my life have melted away and I am a young ten-year-old again. The truth is however, I am staying in someone else's home, I am an adult, and I feel safe and cared for. It feels like I have not even been gone at all. But I am in your spare bedroom, so I feel like I need to go to a hotel."

"Are you crazy? We have enjoyed having you with us and there is no way you are going to a hotel," Donna said.

"I have a spare bedroom," Steven chimed in.

Everyone laughed hysterically while Suzanna lightly punched Steven in his shoulder.

"Ouch," Steven feigned injury and held his shoulder. They all chuckled again as they turned into the driveway.

"Would you like to come in for a bit, Steven?" Donna asked.

"I'd love to, but I have some studying to do this afternoon for my master's degree and a sermon to prepare," he replied. "I'll take a raincheck though."

"Any time, you know you are always welcome," Richard said.

They all shook hands and Steven reluctantly got in his car and drove off while the other three headed inside for the cozy warmth of the family room fireplace, a comfy chair, and another warm cup of hot chocolate with marshmallows.

It didn't take Steven long to pull up in the drive to his parsonage beside the Church building. He was grateful for the comfort of home and being next door to the church he loved so much. There was no denying he was attracted to Suzanna. His wife has been gone more than three years and he was lonely to say the least. He wasn't sure why he felt so drawn to her. They just met. As he briskly walked to the front door with his keys in hand, he noticed a note taped to his front door. He unlocked the door and took the note off the door and laid it on the foyer table as he exited out of his jacket and brown and black plaid scarf. He went into his small office and sat down behind his desk before he opened the 5x7 slip of paper and read the short but not so sweet note.

Pastor, mind your own business. She doesn't need your help. I mean business. Don't make me prove it.

"Well," Steven thought, "that doesn't sound very friendly."

He called Richard and read him the note and they both agreed not to tell Suzanna or Donna and wondered who even knew what was going on much less who cared.

Steven's thoughts would not quit thinking about the threating note and he still had a sermon to finish writing.

When Donna and Suzanna walked in the front door, they got talked into playing a game of Rook. Donna's son, Mike, and the neighbor, Abigail, had been into Monopoly and needed a change of pace. It looks like she may have picked who she may want to go to the Thanksgiving Dance with.

A couple of hours and two cups of hot chocolate with marshmallows later and Suzanna needed to get some rest before supper.

Suzanna went to her room and changed into something casual, called her sister, Debra, and talked almost an hour before laying across the bed and taking a short nap.

That evening, they all retired early since they had to be in court early the next morning. Suzanna did a lot of tossing and turning and didn't get a very restful night of sleep.

Richard was going to go to work instead of going with them to court but in lieu of the turn of events he felt he needed to be with the women, and he felt he needed to tell his wife.

"Why, didn't you tell me last night?" she squealed, but as softly as possible to keep Suzanna from hearing.

"Steven and I thought it was best not to worry the two of you, but I knew if I didn't go to work this morning you would be curious as to why I felt I needed to go," He said with conviction and contrition.

"Richard, we have to tell Suzanna," Donna answered.

"Tell Suzanna what?" Suzanna asked as she walked in the kitchen and caught the tail end of their conversation.

Donna filled her in, and Suzanna was horrified and scared.

"Oh, my," she whispered. "That sounds like a threat."

Steven walked through the kitchen door with a shocked look on his face as he looked from one to the other and pointed toward the living room. "Mike let me in. Richard, I thought we were going to keep this confidential?"

"Well, we were until I decided to go to court with them this morning, and I knew Donna would be suspicious, so I told her when Suzanna walked in," Richard answered in defense.

In unison both Steven and Richard exclaimed, "I felt I needed to be there for them."

"Wonderful then," Donna quipped. "What are we doing standing around? Let's go."

With that said, they all headed to the door and this morning Steven was driving as he headed to his car, and they all followed. He lead Suzanna with a gentle guidance of holding her elbow and opening the front door of his passenger seat. They all drove in silence for the fifteen minutes it took to get downtown to the local courthouse.

Douglas stood outside for them with a folder of paperwork Suzanna gave him and he had a paralegal with him in case he needed her for any grunt work that may need to be done for the case.

Now we will see if Douglas Nightingale is worth the hefty retainer, she paid him the day before. Suzanna's mind could not keep wondering who sent such a nice pastor as Steven such a nasty note.

Chapter 5

The hearing was in a small judge's chamber, and they only waited thirty minutes before being called. Unfortunately, Suzanna and her attorney were the only two allowed inside the judge's chambers. "So much for moral support," she thought to herself. Douglas Nightingale assured her everthing would be fine.

"Please stand for the Honorable Judge John C. Jacobs,"

There were two other people in the judge's chambers aside from Suzanna and Douglas Nightingale, her lawyer. A young lady was the transcriptionist and the court officer making the announcement.

After the judge took his seat, they were allowed to take theirs. A bit formal for just the judge's chambers but it's his show so he makes all the rules.

Douglas Nightingale handed him the last will and testament from Suzanna's grandfather, his death certificate, her mother's death certificate, and her grandfather's sister's death certificate.

"Everything seems to be in order, so what do you need me for?" Judge Jacobs asked.

Douglas stood as he addressed the judge. "Judge Jacobs, the issue is where the inheritance is located—or at the very least where the instructions are to find the inheritance."

"Well Douglas," the judge said, "spit it out. Where is it?"

"Sir, it is buried under her grandmother's headstone right here at the Omaha Heavenly Angels Cemetery.

The judge cleared his throat. "I see no problem with that as long as the casket and the body of course needs to be harmed or touched in any way and you can provide me the proof where this headstone's exact location and plot of the body, etc. Any questions, Douglas?"

"No sir."

"Well, let's give you until Friday around noon to provide me the things I have asked for and shoot for the lifting of the headstone by Monday around 10:00 a.m.," Judge Jacobs said. "Is that agreeable to everybody?"

Douglas Nightingale and Suzanna Johnston both agreed in unison and were dismissed by the court.

When they emerged from the judge's chambers they walked out into the open hallway where Donna and Richard sat on a bench waiting for them.

"Where is Steven?" Suzanna inquired with concern in her voice.

"He was called away for a hospital visit from an elderly member of our congregation," Donna answered. "He fell this morning, broke a leg and bumped his head pretty hard, but he will be fine. He is coming over tonight for supper. He said he would call you to see how everything went."

Douglas shook everyone's hand and excused himself to get to going to work out just fine. "Thank you so much Douglas Nightingale," Suzanna offered.

"Please, call me Douglas. I'll keep you informed as things move along. You guys relax and have a good day."

"Richard and I thought we would drop him off at the office. So, we can go do some shopping and plan what we are going to have for dinner and then pick him up on the way home. Does that sound good?" Donna asked.

Suzanna laughed. "Sure, that sounds pretty good. You know how shopping releases stress. There is just one problem, Steven is the one that drove us here."

"Glad you mentioned that because while you were in the judge's chambers, Steven drove Richard home to pick up our suburban," Donna said.

"Great planning cousin," Suzanna said. "You have thought of everything."

Chapter 5

Three hours later, Suzanna smiled and said, "So glad you thought of this. I have really enjoyed myself. You know, it feels good to be back here in Omaha. I miss all those that we cared for so much."

"Are you planning to visit with anyone else while you are here in town?" Donna asked.

"I am not sure," Suzanna said. "I have mulled it over in my head and my heart. I want to get some resolution to all this mess before I decide. I am weird about it, I guess, but I want the least number of people to know about this until it is all settled."

"I understand and would probably feel the same in your shoes. Speaking of shoes, I know this great shoe store around the corner that sells high end shoes for pennies," Donna said.

"What are we waiting for?" Suzanna asked. "A lady never passes an opportunity for new shoes. Show the way, dear cousin."

Chapter 6

"I had a great afternoon, Suzanna. Thanks for indulging me in a girl's shopping day," Donna said. "To be honest I don't do much outside of family. Richard and I, of course, have some very good close friends. Most of them are from church, and a couple are from work. Outside of dinner out here and there, and church activities, as women without our husbands or outside of Church activities we don't have many special girls' out days.

"I had a wonderful afternoon, too." Suzanna said. "It felt good to get my mind off things, but it feels good to spend time with you after all these years. Which they have just melted away and feels like we have been girlfriends all our lives. So, the feelings are mutual. I have a few close friends and, like you, they all go to my church. Your church reminds me of mine. It is a Christian church as well, and even though it is a large congregation especially coming from a small community. It's not quite as large as yours."

"Since we mentioned church, what do you think of Steven?" Donna asked coyly.

Suzanna blushed. "He is very nice and kindhearted."

"I was shooting for a little more than that," Donna pushed, and she had a big smile on her face.

They had sat down at a little coffee and chocolate shop for a break before heading home.

"What do you mean?" Suzanna asked. "I like him. I am attracted to him if that's what you are asking, but we just met. I don't typically feel this way about someone so quickly so, it troubles me a little. I mean he lives here, and I live in Kentucky. I don't see where a little attraction means anything."

"Oh really?" Donna asked. "Richard and I noticed the chemistry right off. He is very attracted to you as well. He told Richard he can't get you off his mind."

"Really! I mean really," Suzanna corrected.

"Yes, really!" They both looked each other in the eyes and started laughing.

They picked Richard up from work and got home just in time to fix supper before Steven showed up. Suzanna enjoyed working in the kitchen and baked an apple cobbler while Donna fixed a grilled chicken for supper, as well as a salad and steamed vegetables. Steven walked into the kitchen with a basket of flowers.

"For the ladies hard work," he announced. "Heard the good news."

"Still a waiting game, and if it wasn't for Richard and Donna I don't know what I would have done," Suzanna responded.

"Good thing you didn't have to worry about that." He answered.

"Have you found out anything about the note on your front door?" she asked.

"No, but don't worry about that. I am not going to."

Donna looked over at the two of them, thinking how perfectly they were for each other and they both were so hungry for a lasting relationship. Suzanna could move back here. It would be good for her, but it's got to be them making those decisions. She mulled things in her mind before saying, "Suppers on my friends, let's eat."

The home was filled with love and laughter that evening as they ate and shared stories. Mike and Abigail ate with them before going into the living room to play video games.

They retired to the family room after cleaning up the dining room table from supper and stacking the dishes for the dish washer. They were finishing a cup of coffee when Abigail came and thanked Donna for supper.

"I have to be home before 8:30 so I can get ready for bed and school tomorrow," Abigail said. "Good night." She waved three little fingers as she turned to leave. They all told her good night and Mike went upstairs for bed.

Steven decided he needed to get home as well and asked Suzanna if she would walk him to the door.

"Sure," she whispered.

He reached his hand down to help her from her soft, comfy chair and she reached up for it as she looked into his beautiful soft blue eyes that were intently focused on hers.

They walked to the foyer and as he put on his jacket, she couldn't help but admire how handsome he was. He was neatly shaved with dark, wavy hair that always had a curl that was unruly enough to slip down his face and he would take his right hand and softly push it back in place. He smiled when he noticed she was watching him intently.

"I was wondering if you would like to go out to eat tomorrow night. There is this little Italian Restaurant I have been wanting to try out," Steven said.

"Sure, I'd love to." Suzanna accepted without hesitation but wondered what in the world she was doing. With the blink of an eye, he reached out to her and wrapped her in his arms and gave her a gentle kiss that lingered long after it was over. She touched her lips and looked up into his as she melted into his arms and lips, only this time there was no hesitation from either of them. His blue eyes turned dark as he looked at her and released his grip a bit. "I am sorry if I was too forward. I didn't mean for it to…"

She placed two fingers on his lips. "It's okay, I kissed back, didn't I? Which, by the way, I usually don't do before the first date."

They both grinned and began to laugh.

"Tomorrow around 5:30?" he asked.

She nodded, and he walked out the door.

Suzanna was breathless, overwhelmed, and overjoyed. Then she stopped and asked herself "what have I started?"

"Suzanna," Donna called as she walked into the foyer and saw Suzanna leaning against the wall hugging herself.

"I thought I heard the door close. Are you alright?" she asked.

Suzanna nodded her head and then from nowhere tears started to fall and then she sobbed.

Chapter 6

"Suzanna," Donna walked to her and gave her a squeeze and held her until her sobbing ceased. "Let's go get a hot chocolate for a night cap, shall we?" Donna led her into the family room and sat her down on her favorite comfy chair before running to the kitchen to make them both hot chocolate.

Suzanna had dried her tears and was just very quiet when Donna brought in their hot chocolate.

"I am so sorry, I'm just confused." Suzanna explained.

"What did he say or do to make you cry?" Donna asked

Suzanna just spit it out as fast as her lips could speak. "He asked me to dinner tomorrow evening and then he kissed me," Suzanna spit out.

Chapter 7

"I am sorry if he did anything to upset you. He has always been a perfect gentleman," Donna apologized.

"He didn't do a thing wrong, Donna. I kissed him back," Suzanna confessed.

"Then what is wrong, girlfriend?" Donna asked.

Suzanna was quiet for just a moment before she cried out with more tears. "I think I am falling in love with him." She said.

Donna grinned. "And what is wrong with that?"

"Oh Donna, I have only known him for a week," Suzanna said. "My life is in Kentucky, and he is a pastor. I bet there are women from your congregation that are pining for a chance with him."

"And yet it is you he has asked out on a date for the first time since his wife died of cancer three years ago," Donna offered.

"Really?"

"Yes, really," Donna answered with conviction. "Take your time. Nothing has to happen before you both are ready. Have you ever been in a serious relationship?"

"Actually," Suzanna began, "I was engaged a couple of years ago. I am the office manager in a large and prestigious life insurance company. I dated one of the top insurance agents from the office. We got engaged. After two years, I had to fly out to Kansas City for a seminar for some new office equipment. I was gone nearly two weeks. I got home a couple of days early, so I wanted to surprise Edward and didn't tell him. It was around 11:00 p.m. and when I

Chapter 7

walked into my apartment, the lights were on and the music playing. Before I put my bags down, Edward walked out of my bedroom with satin blue boxer shorts on and nothing else."

"How low can a guy get? Why wasn't he at his own place playing around?" Donna asked in disbelief.

"Because he still lived at home with his mommy and daddy," She answered quite seriously until they smiled and looked at each other and started laughing.

"Girl, looks like you dodged a bullet there." Donna managed to spit out. "What happened to the bimbo?"

"The bimbo happened to be my assistant and got pregnant," Suzanna said. "They left the company and moved to Texas. At least that is what I heard. They never showed their faces back at work. I haven't even been on a date since."

"Two years is a long time to not put yourself out there in any way," Donna pointed out.

"I know, but I stay so busy at work. Do you work? Outside of home I mean?" Suzanna asked.

"I volunteer at different church events that we do for the homeless," Donna said. "You wouldn't believe how bad homelessness is here in Omaha."

Donna and Suzanna talked long into the night about everything under the sun. It was as if they had always been best friends. Suzanna was the first to yawn—a good sign they needed to call it a night.

"Are you going to try and see any other family while you are here." Donna asked.

Suzanna thought carefully before answering. "I haven't decided for sure. For one thing, I am not sure if I want to tell anyone else why I am here. At least not until it's over and done. Second, I am not sure who, what, where, and when. So, for now I think it's a no, but I could change my mind at any time. How is everybody? I know I avoided asking, but it isn't that I am not curious or concerned. I'm just guarded, I guess."

"I can understand that. It makes logical sense to me," Donna said.

"I knew you would understand, two peas in a pod thing, right?" Suzanna replied.

Donna nodded in agreement.

"How bad has COVID-19 been here?"

"It was rough for a while," Donna got a little more serious. "Then it got better, but then there was a serious flare up early this winter."

but quickly trickled down. So far, we don't have mask mandates here, and if another variant doesn't flareup we all should be fine. We all got a mild case of it in the beginning and have our antibodies routinely checked. So, if they stay good, we hope vaccine mandates won't affect us either. What about you?"

"Kentucky, and Meade County where I am had it bad twice but Debra, myself, and half my staff at work got it early and we all have our antibodies routinely checked. So far so good and now they have a treatment that can stop it in its tracks, so I am optimistic that we are over the top on this one until something else pops up," Suzanna shared.

"Life is a little crazy sometimes," Donna answered. "Our church never quit in-person services, but we did social distance and wore masks during the worst of it. Most churches stayed open around here. If you didn't feel comfortable going, Steven provided online services and care packages."

Suzanna let out a big yawn, which was followed by one from Donna.

"That's my cue to head to bed," Donna said. "Honestly, it's getting so late I am not sure I will be able to get Richard up for work."

"Where does he work anyway?" Suzanna asked as they stood up and took their cups to put in the sink till morning.

"He is the manager of the local newspaper, *The Omaha Herald*." Donna answered. "He has been manager and editor for more than thirteen years."

"That's great, I love to write. Nothing he would be interested in for print, but I play around with a little photography, too. Just for fun," Suzanna whispered as they had gone upstairs to the bedrooms. "Goodnight and thank you so much for tonight. See you in the morning."

"Night," Donna whispered as she opened her bedroom door and closed it quietly as to not wake up her husband.

Chapter 7

Suddenly they heard a loud crash and Suzanna jumped and bent over as low as she could terrified. Richard flew out of their bedroom and made Donna stay inside as she motioned for Suzanna to come in their room so they would be together.

Richard yelled up to Donna to call the police and for them not to leave the bedroom until the police arrived. Fortunately, their son, Mike, slept through the whole drama but in the morning, he whined that they should have woke him up because he missed all the excitement.

It took the police ten minutes to get there, sirens roaring, waking up the whole neighborhood.

Chapter 8

It was time to get up by the time the police left two and a half hours later. Richard was going to miss another day of work. Fortunately, people these days had laptops, home offices, and cell phones, and were able to at least halfway function at home. He went back to bed for a couple of hours before going to his home office and put in a little time. Donna made Suzanna go to bed for a while and get some rest. She gave Mike a couple pieces of toast and a banana and sent him off to school. After he took a couple of pictures of their front bay window that was shattered in the middle of the night by a big rock. Extreme excitement for a young almost teenager these days. They didn't tell Mike, but the rock had two words written on it, "GO HOME."

The most troubling of all was the fact the words were written in blood.

They all were pretty shaken, but Suzanna was terrified. Donna and Richard told her not to worry about it. She was not going anywhere and it would all be over soon. Richard had already sent the information over to the court from the cemetery and the judge would send the orders for the digging to take place at ten in the morning on Monday.

Suzanna closed her eyes and muffled her sobs so nobody would hear how traumatic this all has been. First Steven, and now her cousin and family had all threatened because of her. She didn't even need that money. She had a good job that paid her more than she needed, but the money could be used to help a lot of other people—family and church friends—but was it worth the risk? Who in the world even knew why she was there or where she was

Chapter 8

to start with. Only three people in Kentucky knew, her sister, brother, and his wife. As far as she knew, very few in Omaha knew who she was, much less why she was there. She got up and took a long, hot, soaking bath and even fell asleep in the tub for a few minutes like she did when she was a kid. After the bath, she laid across the bed and fell asleep for a couple of hours.

It was close to 11:30 a.m. by the time Suzanna dressed and went downstairs. She found Donna cleaning the kitchen. She had a bagel and some juice out for her, but you could tell Donna was either worried, tired, or both.

"Are you okay?" Suzanna asked.

"I'm fine, how about you?"

"I am worried about you guys and what I am doing to your family," Suzanna whispered. "Where's Richard?"

"He actually just went to lay down, after getting a little work sent to his office, and after he picked up all the glass, and after he called Steven for prayer, and after he took care of the people who came to put in a new window." Donna smiled.

"Do you always find a reason to smile?" Suzanna asked.

"Of course! Don't you?" she answered with a grin.

"Most of the time, but this is not one of them," Suzanna confessed. "Oh my, did you say Steven knows about all this?"

"Yes. He does, and he told us to tell you he will see you at 5:30 sharp. So, get some rest this afternoon. His orders not mine." Donna added, "He told us to tell you he is praying for you, too."

"That's sweet," Suzanna said absently.

"Isn't it though?" Donna said, looking at her cousin and new friend. "Are you up for a little drive?"

"I guess so. What's up," Suzanna asked

"There is this little boutique on Old State Boulevard that has the cutest dresses. I think you need something special to wear tonight—my treat. Go get your coat. It won't take long, and I won't take no for an answer. Besides, we can grab something light for lunch while we are out. I'll run and tell Richard or leave a note if he is sleeping."

The little boutique called "The Best Dress in Town" was much bigger than it looked. It stood alone on the corner with its own parking lot and it was busy. Several sales ladies helped other customers, so they were able to look around until Donna found what she was looking for.

"Here, I saw this last week and thought it would look so good on you." She held up a soft, flowing, navy dress that fell below her knees with a pleat down the bodice and full pleats around the skirt. When they zipped it up in the back, it was a perfect fit. Suzanna found a soft, black, faux fur shawl wrap to wear over it and a beautiful pearl necklace and matching earrings to make it a complete ensemble.

"Donna, I love this. You shouldn't though. You have done so much for me already," Suzanna said. "I can't tell you how long it has been since I have bought anything special for a date."

"It is my pleasure. I am having fun vicariously through you," Donna said. "Now let's get us a bite before getting you home and ready for your night out with preacher man."

Donna didn't mention it to Suzanna, but she noticed a black Kia Sport follow them from the boutique to the little pub they stopped at for a bite. When she took notice, the car sped away when the women came out to go home.

Chapter 9

A little after five, Suzanna went downstairs and found the family sitting around the dining room table helping Mike with some nefarious homework.

"Wow Suzanna, you clean up real good," Richard joked. Donna slapped his hand. "I'm serious you look beautiful."

"Thank you." She blushed

Donna spoke up before Prince Charming, Stephen, showed up. "He is correct. You are gorgeous from head to toe." Her green eyes sparkled as she complimented her beautiful cousin.

"Thanks to your help with the window dressing," she offered as the doorbell rang.

Donna spoke up first. "I believe that's for you. Go get him Princess Suzanna. You may stay out as late as you want. A key is under the door mat." Donna winked and Suzanna smiled the sweetest smile Donna had seen in a long time.

Suzanna opened the door and almost melted to the floor at the sight of the most enduring, alluring, handsome man she had seen in a long time. The chemistry between them was almost magical.

"Those are beautiful," She shyly announced. Looking into a dozen yellow roses.

Steven handed them to her as he suggested Donna may have a vase to put them in.

Donna walked around the corner to say hi to Steven and saw the roses. Reading his mind she added, "Let me take those and put them in a vase. I will put them on the desk in your room. You guys need to get going. Have a good evening."

"Thanks Donna," they both said in unison.

He helped her in her seat and helped fasten her seat belt and gave her a peck on the check and her sweet smile told him it was okay.

They drove the short distance to the Italian Job. And pulled up for valet parking. Taking her hand, they walked in and were seated right away in a private little corner where a glass of wine was being pour before they even sat down at the table. He helped her get seated and took her wrap, handing it to the waiter.

They didn't try to carry on a conversation until after they ordered. Finally, they took a deep breath and Suzanna started. "Donna told me Richard called to tell you about the bay window being broken last night."

"Yes, he is an Elder in our church, and I am his pastor. So, if he has a concern or in need of prayer, I am his north star—his go to person. We both needed to cover you in prayer because it is obvious to us someone doesn't want you here or they don't want you to get your hands on your inheritance or don't want you messing with your grandmother's gravestone for some reason."

"I know," Suzanna said. "It is hard to figure who would do such a thing or even who knows I am even here. The only people back home that know are my sister, brother, and sister-in-law."

"Well, there was a little curiosity in the congregation, but I only shared that you were Donna's cousin visiting from Kentucky," he confessed. "Now that we got that out of the way, let's forget about it for the rest of the night."

"I wholeheartedly agree." She smiled at him.

"You light up the whole room when you smile. And you lighten my heart," He offered. "It has been a long time since I have felt this way about anybody. My wife and I were married five years when she passed due to cancer and it has been difficult to move on."

"Have you dated any before now?" She asked.

"Oh, sure. I have tried to put myself out there, but it never felt right to push it. I felt I would know when it was the right time and the right person. I try to allow God to direct my path in all areas of my life."

"So do I." She laughed, and it sounded like music from heaven. "I make less mistakes that way. I was in a relationship for two years that I knew was going nowhere but I couldn't break it off until I found him cheating on me. So, I really haven't taken the time away from my work to even look at anyone, until now. This has come as a big surprise to me."

"And to me," he confessed. "The last thing I was looking for was a relationship right now. You, Susie Q, took me completely by surprise."

Their pasta and salad came and went with only minor chit chat.

"I don't know how you knew, but Italian food is my favorite. I could have lived on spaghetti growing up. My uncle and my mom had contest after contest to see who made the best spaghetti and chili. Meals we often shared when we were together."

"So, who won?" Steven asked.

Suzanna laughed. "Depends on who you asked."

"Was it Donna's family you got together with often?"

"Oh no," Suzanna explained. "Donna's mother and my mother were sisters, but they lived in California when we lived here in Omaha. They moved back to Omaha after their dad became ill with a lung infection from asbestos poisoning. He was a general contractor who built large skyscrapers and I remember a large church when we moved there for about nine months after our grandmother passed away from female cancer. I wonder if it is a coincidence that we moved away from Omaha when my Mom's Mom passed, and Donna's family moved back to Omaha shortly after we moved to Kentucky. Donna's mom and my mom were sisters."

"Pardon my asking, but why isn't Donna part of the inheritance?" Steven asked.

"Different fathers." She explained. "My grandfather came over on a ship from Ireland into New York and was on his way to see his sister when he got sick and stayed the rest of his days in a Catholic hospital and was baptized by nun's before he died. My Mom's Mother Myrtle Mae was a nurse's aide and barely left his side."

"Did he get to see his sister before he died?" He asked

"Oh yes, she spent quite a bit of time with him before he passed. She was a big-time movie producer in Hollywood. At least that's the story I got regarding where her money came from. She didn't like my grandmother and tried to keep her from inheriting any of her money. When my grandmother and her brother married, she couldn't stop it because she never married and had no children."

"So, what did you all think happened to the inheritance?"

"Never gave it a thought. He died young and she lived to a ripe old age and nobody thought anything about it as far as I know. Donna did say that Jason Burns, the man my grandmother was married to when she died, went to her mother and dad and told them some story of Ramona inheriting a bunch of money from her dad but he had been drinking and they didn't think he knew what he was talking about at the time. He died shortly after that. I didn't even hear anything about that until this week."

"Do you mind telling me how much is at stake?" Steven asked.

"Not at all, if I can't trust my pastor who can I trust?" She laughed. "It's approximately eight-six million dollars."

Steven choked on his glass of wine and looked at her to see if she was kidding.

"Yep, you heard it right—eighty-six million dollars. Give or take whatever expenses I'll accrue. Lawyer, etc."

"Wait a minute. What was the name of the man your grandmother was married to when she died?" He asked

"Jason Burns." She answered. "Why?"

"Could he have had any children?"

"No, his only relative was a cousin who had two disabled children and a brother who never married as far as I know. Why?"

"I don't know. That name came up at church a few of weeks ago, but I don't remember why. We have a Christopher Burns in our congregation. I wonder if they could be related. I might do some investigating."

Chapter 9

"You be careful. You don't know what some people will do when it comes to money."

'Yes ma'am, Miss Suzie Q" he joked.

"No joking matter mister," she said.

"What exactly do you intend to do with it?" He asked. "If that's not too personal."

"No, not at all. I'm going to give it away."

"All of it?"

"No, not all of it, but most of it," She answered. "Honest."

"Who are you going to give it to?" he asked.

"I have several charities I am quite fond of. Tunnel to Towers, a couple of children's hospitals, my church has a few special projects they are working on, my sister, brother, a special Christian church here in Omaha, and of course Donna and Richard, but I want it to be a surprise."

The conversation grew to lighter topics until they realized there were only a few tables still occupied, and they both looked down at their watches and noticed how late it was.

"I guess I need to get you home, Susie Q."

She laughed. "I didn't realize it was getting this late. Do you think I broke curfew?"

They both laughed at each other as they looked into each other's eyes and said simultaneously 'I had a good time.'

Chapter 10

Hand in hand, Steven walked Suzanna to the front door and then he took her into his arms gently and looked into her eyes as she looked up into his for just a moment before they both bent forward for a long, soft, intimate and gentle kiss. There was more passion in that one kiss than she had ever experienced in all her past relationships gathered together into one. Neither of them wanted the night to end, and they held onto the embrace a little longer before Suzanna said she needed to go. Steven bent over to get the key that was hidden under the door mat and handed it to Suzanna. Their fingers touched, and when she looked up into his eyes, they kissed another lingering kiss like the scent of a beautiful rose that lingered long after it was gone.

"I had an amazing time tonight, Susie Q."

"So did I," Suzanna replied. "It's hard to let it go."

"Yes, it is," he answered. "Suzanna." He took both hands into his and looked into her angelic eyes.

"Yes," she responded looking up into his.

"I have fallen in love with..."

She placed two of her fingers against his lips to quiet him. "Me too." She finished and reached her lips to his and ended their evening with a warm embrace as he unlocked the door for her, and she went inside floating on a cloud.

She took off her shoes before climbing the stairs to her bedroom and fell into the bed exhausted but happier than she had ever felt. Life had taken

CHAPTER 10

a turn toward uncharted territory. She suddenly realized for the first time in her life that she was really in love. She fell asleep with a grin on her face, peace in her heart, and a prayer on her lips.

SATURDAY

Suzanna lingered in bed, listening to the Saturday morning activity below since the whole family waws at home. She didn't get up for breakfast. She felt like snuggling under the covers with the soft sweet memories of her night with Steven fresh on her mind. The beautiful yellow roses provided a soft scent of love that circulated throughout the bedroom as Donna had put them in a beautiful green and coral vase that matched the bedroom décor and just the scent itself with eyes closed reminded her of their date the night before.

She heard a soft peck at her bedroom door.

"Suzanna? Are you up?" Donna inquired.

"Come in, Donna," she replied.

Donna peeked her head in through the door, and Suzanna laughed. "Please, come in." She opened the door wide enough to slither through and went to the desk and pulled out the chair and sat down. "Well, cousin?"

"Well, what?" she laughed.

"You know what, silly! How'd it go?" Donna pried.

Suzanna laughed and threw the covers over her head, then peeked her eyes over the top. "Amazing, everything went well. For the first time in my life, I am in love!" She squealed.

"Fill me in, silly. I want details," Donna demanded. "I am so happy for you. I suppose he is in love to?"

"Yes, yes, and yes. Oh Donna, am I dreaming or is this for real?"

"I think it is, yes."

"Steven called Richard this morning and they prayed together over your relationship and his feeling he is in love with you and they both got off the phone feeling reassured. He really cares for you "Susie Q."

"The church rented the outdoor ice-skating rink at Lincoln Park. Did you want to tag along?"

"Is that where they have fireworks on the Fourth of July?" Suzanna asked.

Donna laughed. "One of the many places these days. We always go to Louisville Lake where Uncle Dale liked to go fishing, and we would have big family picnics there."

"Oh, I remember. We went fishing almost every weekend at Louisville Lake when we were kids. Robert and I loved to fish. The rest of the kids just played kid games."

"Get you motor running. We will be leaving in about an hour. Dress warm."

1:30 p.m.

There was a big crowd already there by the time they pulled into the parking lot of the park. It wasn't too cold out. Suzanna thought how cold it felt a week ago around the same time. She had made it to Omaha, and it snowed off and on for a few days before she got there. There were only flurries at the time, but she wasn't used to the cold and a northern wind kept it a few degrees colder. However, after a week she had begun to get use to the weather, and it really wasn't that bad. She loved Omaha winters growing up. Compared to Kentucky's. Everyone liked snow for Christmas, didn't they? Steven was already skating and was skating with three little girls who needed a little help and encouragement. Once she got her skates on, she grabbed the hand of the last one holding on and they skated for thirty minutes with the little ones before they got bored and went to get something to drink and some popcorn with their parents. There were small tables all around the ice. Once the little ones left, Steven took Suzanna's hand and they skated around the large ice rink together. They were both pretty good skaters, so they skated with little effort and playfully meandered around—backward and forward—and skated to a waltz like they were dancing. With a sly grin, Steven pecked her on the cheek with a kiss—being careful to be a gentleman and recognizing he was the 'pastor at the event. They decided to take a break. While working their way to the edge of the rink, someone bumped hard into Suzanna and knocked her off her feet. She hit her head on the ice and it knocked her out for a short time. When she woke up, a paramedic had a cold cloth on her forehead, and they were loading her in an ambulance. When she tried to protest they said since she lost consciousness, so it was a precaution. Steven assured her he would be there shortly.

4:10

When Steven got to Omaha General Hospital, he was informed that no one from the park was ever brought there. He argued with them to no avail until Donna and Richard showed up to add their two cents.

"We demand to see security." Donna's voice got louder. "A paramedic and ambulance came for her and told us this was where they were bringing her."

5:15

The police showed up and took a report and told them there wasn't any more they could do there. They would call when anything new came up.

Suzanna woke up in the dark. She had been drugged but was in the ambulance strapped down.

"I warned you to go back to where you belong," spoke a deep voice from somewhere in the darkness.

She tried to speak but realized she was gagged and couldn't respond. She had something over her head and that was why it was so dark.

Whoever it was took the gag out of her mouth, but she still couldn't see. "Who are you and what do you want with me?" She cried.

"That money belongs to me," the gruff voice hurled at her. "You don't deserve any of it. It should have been mine."

Suzanna tried to hold it together. "I don't want it. I was going to give most of it to charity anyway. Just tell me who you are, and I'll be glad to share it with you."

"Sure, you will," he laughed. "I don't want to hurt you. I just want you to go home. Please do what I ask, or somebody will get hurt." He placed a cloth over her nose and mouth, and she passed out.

8:24

The police found the ambulance behind the hospital. It was parked and locked, and just left there. When they got it open, Suzanna was there—gagged and tied up and only slightly conscience. They rushed her into the hospital, but the only injury found was the cut on her forehead from her fall at the ice-skating rink. They called the pastor of the event and her cousin Donna. They all got there in record time, but they had her admitted upstairs for observation considering the probability of a concussion, especially being drugged . She told the police everything she could remember, and they relayed it to the family—cautioning them not to press her for more information until morning. They wanted the drugs to have time to get out of her system, hoping she would be able to remember a little better.

Donna spoke up first. "I am not leaving her side."

"I am not leaving her side either," Steven added.

The police looked at Richard." I am going home and going to bed." They all looked at him and laughed.

The police officer said, "Smart man. My shift is over, so I think that's what I am going to do too. I'll be back in the morning to see if she remembers anything else and to make sure she is okay to go home. If you all need anything before you see me in the morning, here is my card, badge number, and my name Officer Jacobs. Good night, folks."

Chapter 11

Suzanna briefly woke to give Steven and Donna a big smile then drifted back to sleep. Around 4:30 a.m., Donna woke Steven. He was slumped over Suzanna's bed with both hands cupped over her one hand and his head peacefully lying in her lap.

"Steven, you need to wake up." Donna pleaded.

Steven raised up. "What? What's wrong?"

"Nothing's wrong," Donna whispered. "I just thought you needed to go home and get cleaned up for church."

"What time is it?" He asked.

Donna looked down at her watch. "It's around 4:30."

"Yeah, I guess you're probably right. Can you hold down the fort till after church?"

"You know I can and will. Now go and get a little rest—if that's possible."

He raised up and brushed an unruly curl out of his face that Suzanna thought was so cute. "Call me if anything comes up or you need anything."

She nodded okay as he tip-toed out the door, which was slightly ajar so he could quietly slip out undetected even though Suzanna was beginning to get a little restless. It was almost two hours later when Suzanna woke up and saw Donna curled up with a blanket sound asleep in the adjacent recliner. Momma Bear at her post for a long winter nap. Suzanna thought to herself with a grin. Her head hurt and she remembered a nurse had told her she was going to have a headache for a bit.

Donna woke to a noise in the hallway and saw Suzanna looking at her. "Good morning cousin." She offered.

"Good morning to you. Did Steven go home?" She asked.

"I made him go get cleaned up before church," Donna replied.

"Oh no, I completely forgot it's Sunday. Do you think they might let me go?"

"No, I don't. You are going to need to get some rest with that concussion and all you have been through," Donna answered, standing up and looking at the bump on her forehead.

"It doesn't hurt too bad," She bravely offered.

"Sure, it doesn't. It just looks horrendous. The whole side of your face is purple," Donna added. "The police officer said he would be by this morning to take your official statement. The hospital was protective of you and your rights last night."

"Good morning, ladies," said Gloria, a nurse's assistant. "I just have to get your vitals before breakfast gets in here. I hope it is okay Miss Donna, I had them bring you up a complimentary tray with Miss Suzanna's."

"Thank you," Donna said. "I am a bit hungry."

"Me too!" Suzanna chimed in while she had a thermometer dangling out of her lips.

Chapter 12

Even though the morning slowly went by, she stayed rather busy. After her and Donna ate breakfast, a couple of neurologists came in to see her and explained how serious her concussion was and if she wanted to leave the hospital it was imperative, she get plenty of rest and if she remembers anything she needs to let them know as soon as possible. Plenty of rest, plenty of fluids. Be careful to not let your head get knocked on anything for a while.

After the neurologists left, Suzanna was so tired she took a short nap while Donna read a few articles from *Time* magazine. At 11:00, using Donna's iPad, they watched Steven preach one of his best sermons. Donna and Suzanna both grinned ear to ear.

"That's the best sermon I have ever heard come out of that man's mouth," Donna offered.

"I have only heard one other sermon," Suzanna mentioned, and that one other sermon will stick with me forever. As will this one. The message was spot on about forgiveness and coveting what does not belong to you.

"I must agree, it was a good message," said Sargent Owen Matthews as he walked into her hospital room.

"Good morning, sergeant," Suzanna and Donna greeted in unison and looked at each other and got tickled enough to laugh out loud. At each other. They were extremely tired and would probably laugh at anything.

"How are you doing young lady?" Sergeant Matthews asked.

"I'm doing good, except I still have a headache," Suzanna answered.

"I wondered if you were up to answering a few questions."

"Sure, whatever I can do to help," she offered.

"Did he say anything or what was his overall demeaner? Was he abusive?"

"I don't remember, really I don't." Suzanna appealed to them both, "at least not a lot. He just told me my inheritance belonged to him and his family and I told him I don't want the money I was just going to give it away to charities. That seemed to make him mad, and he put a cloth over my face. I woke up here. He did say he didn't want to hurt anyone, but he would do whatever he had to."

"That's okay doll we just had to ask. But that was a little help right there. See, you remember more than you think, and I'll bet more will come back to you in a couple of days. Like, what he looks like and where he took you, things like that. We really don't expect you to remember anything this soon, but as soon as it comes to you, we don't want you to tell anyone until we are notified, okay. You understand, don't you?"

"Yes sir, I do." Suzanna nodded.

Soon after church service, Richard and Mike arrived at the hospital, along with Steven, to check if the girls were able to leave the hospital so they all could go to lunch. Steven brought a big gift box tied with a pretty, pink and blue ribbon. He handed it to Suzanna and bent down across her bed to give her a peck on the check. For being in the hospital, she was certainly glowing.

"What's this?" Suzanna asked.

"Some of the ladies from church got together and put a get-well box together of some things you may or may not have while you are here. There are a few things from Donna, too. She looked up at everybody and a few tears momentarily blurred her vision. You all are so great. I don't know how to thank you.

"Open quick, Mike is a starving young man,: Richard said with a big grin.

She slowly opened the big box and inside was a big fluffy black and olive-green scarf with matching gloves. and a stuffed brown and black gorilla.

"That's from me," Steven added. A study Bible and a Christian crossword puzzle book, an adult Christian coloring book and some markers. A couple of books to read written by Max Lucado and a Bible Study by Beth Moore.

"How did you all know two of my all-time favorites?" She asked as she looked up at everyone.

CHAPTER 12

"Oh, we have our ways," Steven answered.

Richard had stepped out of the room but walked back in long enough to tell everyone the good news. "The farthest we can take Miss Prissy is to the cafeteria but if she does well, she can go home." They all let out a big cheer before being reminded they were in a hospital with sick people.

They enjoyed a good lunch with a lot of conversation and laughter. Donna could tell Suzanna was getting tired, so as soon as she finished eating, she recommended going back to her room to get a little rest and she readily agreed.

The doctor came in shortly after, and in spite of her downtrodden expression thought it best to stay in one more night. She agreed, if she could leave early. Tomorrow was the day they were going to lift her grandmother's headstone and see where it led, and she needed to be there.

The family left, but Steven stayed to have a private visit. They enjoyed the afternoon together and he did not miss the opportunity to kiss her beautiful warm lips as gently as possible and she felt like this must be what Heaven must be like. To be loved and cherished in a way where no words could explain it is how special she felt in his arms. God's love is indescribable. Maybe love itself is not meant to be described but experienced, enjoyed, and accepted. A precious gift.

Suzanna fell asleep in his arms as he lay beside her in the hospital bed. No words were spoken just experienced the joy of being together. She woke up and it was dark, and she was alone, but Steven left her a note on her lap. As she opened the note, she smiled sweetly at the tender nick name he had given her.

Susie Q,

I had some church business to attend to so, I needed to go. I didn't want to disturb your beauty sleep. I will be here early in the morning to pick you up for the cemetery. No matter what happens, I will be here for you. Get plenty of rest dear heart. I am counting the moments.

All my love,
Steven

Chapter 13

Donna was there before Steven and helped Suzanna get dressed. She bought her some warmer clothes, a heavier coat, and a classic pair of black boots. Steven provided the rest, her new gloves and the black and olive scarf. As soon as she was dressed it was as if on cue Steven walked through the door.

"Where's Richard?" he asked. He hugged Donna and placed a soft kiss on Suzanna's cheek.

"He is meeting us there. Our lawyer and the judge are going to be present in case anything comes up," Donna answered.

"Well, are we ready?" Donna asked. She looked at Steven and knew there was one more thing to be done.

As they held each other's hands and had a time of prayer. Offering up concerns from each of them and the praises along with anything any one of them needed to bring up. Finally, Suzanna spoke up to pray for the one who kidnapped her. That God would forgive him and bring him peace and come out in the open so they could handle the issue head on as fellow Christians, in love and forgiveness as Jesus would. They all agreed. Looking at one another, Suzanna said, "Let's do this." They all smiled, hugged, and walked out the door.

As they made their way toward the cemetery, there was little conversation. They were all lost in their own thoughts. When they turned into the cemetery, Suzanna saw what a large cemetery it was. The different streets were numbered and named, and in the middle of the massive cemetery was

Chapter 13

a giant gazebo. A donation from a prominent resting home for someone special, Suzanna supposed.

Finally, they reached their destination. Two beautiful weeping willow trees, a couple of benches, a few bushes and a piece of heavy equipment. Channel 4 news van and a reporter and camera and a few distinguished gentlemen ended the procession of important and not so important people who were there to watch her grandmothers resting place become an invasion. Suzanna suddenly felt she was wrong for doing this, but what choice did she have? The voice of the one who knew what she should do echoed in her mind. "Go home. Go home. Go home, where you belong." She began to think he was right.

As soon as she stepped out of the suburban, a microphone was shoved into her face. Miss Johnson, how do you feel about this total disrespect for the grave of your grandmother. Steven stepped in front of Suzanna. "Miss Suzanna Johnson has no comment at this time."

"That's okay, I don't mind," Suzanna said. "I am not thrilled with any of this, but we are following her wishes and what needs to be done and nothing more and it will be over."

"We heard you were kidnapped. How are you feeling?" the young, blonde reporter asked.

"I feel fine. Thank you for asking." Suzanna replied.

Steven then took her by her waist and led her closer to where the digging had already begun and out of reach from the reporter and cameras.

They gently lifted the headstone up and off and sat it down away from harming anything or anyone. The operator was a true professional.

Two police detectives, the judge, and the lawyer were beside the small crater in the ground and the two detectives pulled out a black, shiny, metal box and sat it down in front of the judge and Douglas who handed the judge two large keys. Judge Jacobs, with everyone's eyes on the box, put both keys in at once and simultaneously turned them. The lid opened and without further ado, he reached in and pulled out the papers and handed them over to their lawyer the legal representative of the legal heir.

The police dismissed the crowd that had gathered even the curiosity seekers who just stumbled across something they knew nothing about.

They were all waiting at Douglas' office for more than a half hour when he walked in the side door with his big brown leather satchel carrying his black wool coat over his left arm and Cynthia followed him into his office carrying a couple sticky notes attached to two of her fingers on her left hand. She then told them all they could join him in the meeting room.

As they walked in, he had already pulled the papers from his satchel and scanned them. Steven pulled out a chair for Suzanna and Richard pulled out a chair for Donna.

He went straight to business. "I have a note from the police detective who took care of you at the hospital for me to call as soon as I got here. We barely spoke a minute. I told him I would call him back later, but he called to inform me that the man who kidnapped you, Suzanna, is dead. He shot himself in the head early this morning. His name is Jason Burns and was some relation to the husband of your grandmother when she died is 1964. He never married and the only living relative who was still living. He left a note to apologize for what he did and remarked that you only tried to show kindness despite how he treated you. When I get more, I'll let you know."

"Is everybody doing okay and ready to move on?" Douglas asked. He was certainly in his element and commanded the respect he was often given. The four of them were a bit shell shocked and quiet as mice. Affirmative head nodding was the only response he got from them, so he continued.

"From what I have seen so far, this is a self-explanatory will. With all the proper paperwork you all have shown me so far, Miss Suzanna Johnson is soul heir. There is only one tiny thing different." He waited for a response.

Richard was the one who spoke up first. "What's wrong?" he asked.

"Oh, nothing's wrong—not at all. It's just that the eight-six million dollars she has inherited was the amount before interest on the estate was accrued."

He picked up his phone. "Yes, Cynthia do you have that figure for us yet? Umm, alright, good, good. Thank you, Cynthia. Yes of course, take the rest of the day off. Yes, you are welcome."

Chapter 13

"According to Cynthia's calculations, that makes the true value approximately two-hundred forty-six million dollars."

They all sat back in their seats in shock.

Chapter 14

They were quiet on the drive home. Richard went to work and Donna and Suzanna rode with Steven to Waffle House for a bite to eat.

Steven broke the silence. "Well Suzie Q, how does it feel to be a millionaire?"

"So far, it still doesn't feel real," she answered. "When I actually hold some of it in my hand, then I may believe it."

With stomachs full of pancakes, waffles, and hash browns and conversation all about what one would do with all that money Suzanna finally spoke up, "That poor man. All alone in the world and then unable to live with things he had done, felt too painfully guilty to live with himself."

"I know how you must feel Suzie Q, but it is a relief not to worry about him coming after you again—at least for us," Steven said looking at himself and Donna.

Suzanna bent her head and cried. Steven lay his hand on her shoulder. She looked so vulnerable, so tender hearted, a generous and loving spirit. How could he not have fallen in love with her? Donna looked at him and their eyes met. She knew exactly what he was thinking and feeling and was overwhelmed with emotion herself. She watched him suffer when his wife passed away. That had been difficult.

This tenderness between them was joyful yet subdued because of all the many other things going on between them, around them, and with them. All great love stories have a beginning, a present, and a forever after. She prayed this one had a good forever after. They both deserved one.

Chapter 14

When Donna and Suzanna hit the inside of the front door, they both said, "I'm exhausted." Laughed and announced in unison as they so often do, "I'm going to lay down for a while."

Donna fixed supper and Suzanna heard dishes rattling around in the kitchen. She had been up for quite a while and decided to pick up one of the books they had all given her to read. It didn't take up long to read nearly a third of the way through it. It was about a young, Amish girl who decided to go off on her own and became a Christian and is now falling in love with her pastors' son. Good reading, Suzanna thought to herself.

She stood up and stretched long and tall and went to wash her hands when she realized something was missing and walked back into the bedroom and there it was. Her beautiful bouquet of yellow roses were nowhere to be seen. Donna had placed them in that beautiful coral glass vase.

After she sat the table and was working on getting the potatoes mashed, she asked Donna about them.

"Of course not silly, why would I?" Donna replied and looked into Suzanna's eyes.

"Because they are no longer in my room," Suzanna said.

As if on cue, Richard walked in the front door.

Donna announced, "Supper's ready! Come and get it while it's hot."

Supper was so good everyone overindulged a bit. The conversation was light until the roses came up again.

"I looked everywhere, up down and all around." She said jokingly. "I just don't want anything happening to your vase.

"Oh, that ol' thing? No worries about that. Just the mystery where they could have gone," Donna said.

"Are you guys talking about the yellow roses Steven gave Suzie Q?" Richard teased.

"Yes of course, love." Donna replied to her husband. "Why, have you seen them?"

"Well, yes. The roses were in the sink Saturday and the vase was broken and laying on a paper towel on the counter. Since the roses wilted quite a bit,

I threw them out when I got the trash ready to take to the curb. Was that okay?" He replied, worried he had done something wrong.

"Of course, it is sweetheart. We just didn't know what had happened to them is all. But I wonder how the vase got broken to start with," Donna said. She and Suzanna looked at each other, worried another mystery was about to unfold.

"Well," Mike chimed in, "I'm sorry. I didn't mean to do anything wrong but there was a book in the gift box the church gave Suzanna that I thought about reading. One of my friends had read it, and you guys were gone with Suzanna in the hospital and everything, so I let myself in her room. I'm so sorry."

"Mike, you didn't do anything wrong so please think nothing of it. Okay?" Suzanna tried to reassure him. "What book did you want to read?

"I don't remember the name of it, but I must have been mistaken because I couldn't find it in the box. It was about a young Amish girl that becomes a Christian."

Suzanna laughed. "It's under my pillow where I stash the book I am currently reading while lying in bed. I should finish it by morning and it's all yours."

They all chuckled in relief that another was mystery solved.

After dishes were finished, they got a cup of hot chocolate and a bag of mini marshmallows and sat in the family room for a couple of hours before one by one they meandered towards going to bed.

True to her word, Suzanna stayed up long enough to finish the book, *A Shepherd's Journey*. Millie, the young Amish girl, set off a chain of events one Christmas and the story grew to be more about the pastor of The Little Flock Church than it was about the young girl. All in all, it brought out an important thing about life in general. We do not walk this journey called life all alone. We touch the lives of others and others touch our lives. If we strive to live a life like Christ, we just might touch people in positive, loving, and helpful ways, and we are less likely to hurt others along our path.

After finishing the book, she couldn't sleep so she spent a little time in God's word and then journaled and reflected on her own journey and what

Chapter 14

she was going to do. Where would God lead her? What did he want her to do with the rest of her life? Where did Steven fit in? Would her journey take her on a whole new path? All Suzanna knew was she had a lot of decisions to make and some of them would affect the lives of others. Suzanna and God had a lot of talking to do and she had a lot of listening to do if she wanted to find the right answers.

Does that mean she should listen to her heart? Too soon to tell. Now that things have settled down a bit, maybe a little self-reflection and fun could be enjoyed. A chance for her and Steven to get to know each other a little better, it would be great to spend the holidays here. Maybe see if her sister could come and spend the holidays back in Omaha just like when we were kids. As she started to doze off, she decided to talk to Donna about it in the morning.

Chapter 15

Mike had already left for school and Richard for work when Suzanna went down and found Donna getting ready to do a load of wash and asked Suzanna if there was anything she needed cleaned. She had already cleaned the kitchen and left a bagel and a blueberry muffin for Suzanna to nibble on as she fixed her a cup of hot chocolate. As was beginning to become their routine they sat at the table for their morning girl chat.

Donna mentioned Mike's excitement for the upcoming Thanksgiving dance and his first date which was with his neighbor and video game buddy, Abigail.

"Thanksgiving is still a bit in the future," Suzanna mentioned.

"Yes, but they don't wait till that close to the holidays because of vacations and holiday shopping," Donna explained. "You may not realize it, but this Saturday will be November 2. We have been asked to be chaperones. As is Steven as well. I wonder who he'll ask to chaperone with him?" She grinned at Suzanna.

"I haven't heard anything about it. He may have already asked someone," Suzanna deflected. Nervously hoping he hadn't.

"Well, I have it on good authority that he hasn't," Donna responded.

Suzanna's cell phone rung.

Suzanna hung up the phone from Steven. "He wants me to go to lunch with him around one."

"Sounds like fun. Where to?" Donna asked.

"He didn't say."

Chapter 15

"Oh, I forgot Douglas called this morning and said your funds should be available tomorrow if you wanted to go around eleven tomorrow. You can go over your wishes for the different charities, the bank to make your deposits, savings etc," Donna said. "Do you know what you are going to do when you become filthy rich?"

Suzanna laughed. "Yeah, forget I have any money. Donna, is there anything special you guys need or want, or anything I can do for you guys?"

"Not a thing, silly." Donna laughed. "I can't think of anything important enough to mention."

"I want to do something special for you. Your family has been so supportive. I don't know what I would have done without you." Suzanna teared up a little and she dried a tear with a tissue Donna gave her.

"We haven't done anything a cousin wouldn't do for another. We are family, and I for one am happy you are here. Do you know what your plans are going forward? You know you are welcome here as long as you want. We have all enjoyed your visit. Minus the intrigue, however." She laughed. "Especially a young Pastor we both know."

"I have been thinking about that, and want to talk to you about it," Suzanna said.

Donna jumped in. "Yes, yes, and yes!"

"Yes, yes and yes what?" Suzanna asked her bewildered.

"It doesn't matter the answer is yes, you silly goose. You can move in permanently if you want," Donna replied. "What would Steven think of me if I didn't agree?"

"I actually want to prolong my trip here through the holidays, and I've even thought about asking Deb if she wants to join me here for Christmas."

"That's a wonderful idea! We have a few extra rooms in the basement. We use the big, open, floor plan for holiday get-togethers. The spare bedrooms the kids use when they were staying over."

Suzanna continued. "I feel like the extra time would give Steven and me more time to get to know each other and for me to consider if I want to move here."

"Oh Suzanna, that would be amazing! We would all love it. Really, we would. As for Steven, we already know you two are meant to be together." Looking down at her watch she added, "Speaking of the devil, you need to get ready for your lunch date."

Suzanna looked down at her watch. "Oops, I didn't realize it was getting so late. I finished that book last night and set it on Mike's nightstand. His bedroom door was open. He keeps a clean bedroom for a teenage boy!"

Donna laughed. "Only when mom goes in early in the morning and gives it a good cleaning. That's why the door was left open. Trust me when I say I wouldn't have left it open if I left it the way I found it."

They stood up and hugged each other tight. Both appreciating the friendship they both enjoyed from one another. Donna whispered, "Enjoy your date."

Chapter 16

Suzanna heard voices downstairs which probably meant Steven had arrived for lunch/dinner depending on what part of the country you were from. She changed her outfit three times and knew Donna would give her as much time as she needed without rushing her. She finally settled on a blue-ish gray pair of suit pants and a long-sleeve, matching blouse that hung below the waistline with a doubled ruffle and white trim around the v neck collar and a simple pearl necklace with matching pierced earrings. The stairs creaked on the third to the bottom step, announcing to the pair waiting in the family room that she was ready.

She entered the room, greeted by smiles and she returned a smile back to the only eyes she saw that melted her heart every time she met them.

Steven was entranced with her and could barely speak. She always entered a room with such grace and elegance. "Beautiful as always Suzie Q."

"I didn't know what to wear because I'm not sure where we're going. Does this look okay?" She asked as she straightened the invisible to everyone else but her wrinkles from coming down the stairs.

"Perfect," both Steven and Donna replied before Suzanna spoke up, "We do that a lot. Maybe Donna just knows exactly what everyone is going to say before they say it."

"You two get out of my hair, so I can get some work done." Donna laughed.

They walked toward the front door and Donna opened it. She gave Suzanna a mild hug and told them both to have a good afternoon.

They went to a little mom and pop restaurant on the east side of the city. Past the busy downtown and into a more rural area with lots of farmland. It was a simple yet elegant very private place. A comfortable paved parking lot surrounded by trees. If you didn't know it was there you would miss it altogether. Steven helped her out of the car, and they walked toward the door. The sign read, A Little Piece of Irish Heaven and had a rainbow and a pot of gold beside it.

"Wonderful," Suzanna quietly said as Steven guided her to the front door. "I thought you might like this. I have been here a few times, but I love the food. And the people who own it go to our church."

When they walked in the door, someone named Sheila asked if she could take their coats. Steven helped Suzanna out of her winter coat, and handed them both to Sheila. Andrea greeted them and Andrea came to take their order. The dining room was beautiful with a large stone fireplace in the middle that serviced a warm soft ambiance for the whole dining room which gave the appearance of a circular eating arrangement. Their table was in a little nook close to the warmth of the fire. The tables were all dressed in a pale soft color of green and candlelight came from a pot of gold. The chairs were ivory with a soft green cushioned bottom you practically melted into when you sat down. Two sparkling glasses of ice water awaited them as Sheila sat them and asked if they needed anything else to drink. Suzanna looked to Steven for guidance.

"Yes, we would like a glass of white wine please."

"Certainly, sir," she replied.

She was still admiring how beautiful and authentic of a replica of a real Irish pub. The wall had various pictures of beautiful Ireland—her grandfather's homeland. Suzanna sat and admired, but when she looked at Steven her eyes filled with tears just thinking about how amazingly wonderful he is to be so thoughtful to bring her here.

"My dear, don't you like it?" Steven asked.

"Of course, I love it. I was just thinking of how thoughtful you are to bring me here. It has always been my dream to one day go to Ireland and find where my grandfather was raised and if he had any family left there."

Chapter 16

"Maybe one day you will." Steven was thoughtful. "Maybe someday we will go together."

Sheila number three came to take their order as they both carried on about the décor when the owner of the restaurant came to say hi. "Pastor Landry, how is everything this afternoon? Everyone doing a good job of taking care of you?"

"The service here is impeccable, Shawn. How is your wife doing?" Steven asked.

"She is recovering well. We will both probably be at church on Sunday," Shawn answered.

"Shawn, I'd like you to meet Suzanna Johnson. She's the young lady I mentioned to you. Her grandfather is from Ireland."

"Yes, of course. Nice to meet you, young lady. What was your grandfather's name? I might know some of his family."

"His full name was Jamie McMurtry. I never met him. He died due to stomach cancer when my mother was five years old," Suzanna said.

"Yes, I see. You know, I do know where the McMurty's began. Maybe I can ask around and see if anyone knows of him or his family," He offered.

"That's very kind of you. Thank you for offering."

"No problem, Miss. I'm going to let you two have some privacy to enjoy your meal. It should be out shortly."

After a few minutes of chit chat, their lunch came out piping hot, juicy, and tender. Venison and potatoes like she had never eaten before and ended with homemade peach cobbler.

"That was an amazing meal," Suzanna said.

"I'd like to agree on that." Steven said before bringing up a personal question he was afraid to ask. "Now that the estate is settled, and you are to get the funds dispersed tomorrow, what is your plan?"

"I wanted to talk to you about that. I talked it over with Donna, and I'll stay with her through the holidays. I want to ask my sister to come up and visit as well. How do you feel about that?" Suzanna asked.

"Are you kidding? I love that idea! Christmas use to be such a happy time for me but since my wife died, I haven't been in a festive mood around Christmas," Steven told her. "What will you do after the holidays?"

"Part of that depends on us, I guess. If things continue to go well and if I can find work of some kind, I will buy my own place here," she said. "If you think what we have together is real and want me to stay, I would love to stay."

"I am certain what we have is real. You don't have to know someone for any certain length of time to know how you feel about them, and I know I am falling in love with you. Miss Suzanna Johnson. I am so glad you are considering a move back here. My church wouldn't like it if I sent them a sermon from Kentucky every week because as you already know, being a pastor and a pastor's wife is a lot more than just preaching sermons. They both laughed and Steven reached across the table to hold her hand then raised it to his lips and tenderly kissed each finger. Her heart melted and they stayed there for another hour before deciding they needed to get home.

When he pulled into the driveway at Donna's house, he walked around the door, opened it and helped her out but before they walked to the front door, he wrapped her in his arms and kissed her passionately then looked into her eyes and whispered, "I don't ever want to let you out of my arms."

Then another peck before turning and walking her up to the front door.

"Thank you, Steven, for such a wonderful afternoon."

"The pleasure, Suzie Q, is all mine."

Steven turned to walk away when she grabbed his arm and softly whispered, "Please don't go, not yet."

"I have to, my love. I have pastor duties today." And with that, he was at his car trembling because he did not want to leave her. Started the engine and gazed up at her one last time as she was walking in the door, he drove off alone and lonely.

Chapter 17

As Suzanna and Donna left the lawyers office, they both let out a large sigh of relief that this part of the journey was over. Sitting in Donna's Suburban, looking over the paperwork, checking and savings, and a new IRA Account they both laughed when they saw the cost of her lawyer's fees.

"Well, Douglas became a quick millionaire. Can you imagine if his brother Jamison had been the lawyer in charge?" Donna commented. "The fee would at least be double. I guarantee it."

"I'd like to go by the bank if there is one close by, and then I want to go shopping for some new clothes." Suzanna giggled. "I feel like a young schoolgirl."

She left the bank, sat back in the car seat, and handed Donna a cashier's check made out to her and Richard for two million dollars.

"What in the world is this?" Donna asked.

"It is something I have been wanting to do for you all. I know you don't really need it, but I am sure you can find a use for it.," Suzanna told her.

"Of course we can, but sweetie you didn't have to do this," Donna said.

"Yes, I know. But I wanted to and I'm so glad it turned out like this. So, can we go shopping now?" Suzanna asked.

They shopped until they dropped, and for the most part it was all clothes. When they got back in the car, Donna spoke up. "Do you care if I show you something before, we head home."

"Sure, not at all, I am at your mercy." Suzanna laughed.

They drove toward Donna's subdivision but turned left instead of right and after five minutes Donna stopped in front of a gated home with stone pillars along both sides of a large ornate iron gate and as she pushed a small blue button the gate opened in the middle for which they drove through. Once through the gates, they closed and it was as if they entered another beautiful and peaceful world. A short concrete driveway lined with beautiful weeping willow trees until the drive ended in front of a beautiful brick home with stone accents toward a courtyard on the left.

"Donna, what's this?"

"A friend of mine lived here. She moved to Paris where her job led her. Fell in love married and has had a tiny little girl they named 'Paris' after the country where they fell in love. She has been trying to sell it for two years. There is not a huge demand for such a place as this around here, but it is a warm, lovely home, and I have lots of good memories here. I just thought about it and decided to show you. I called Felicia and told her about you, and she sent me all the information and the keys to everything, so we can look around at our leisure. There is no realty company, only a close friend who is handling her affairs here in the states. What do you think?" Donna finally asked.

"It's … it's beautiful, Donna. It really is, but am I ready? What if things don't work out with Steven?" Suzanna was excited but overwhelmed. She didn't want to make decisions this soon that would affect her whole life.

"Sweetie, we are just going to look. No hasty decisions, just a look, and then something to think about. Okay?" Donna knew her well enough that she just shot her way past her comfort zone but that is why she approached it now. This way she can mull it over, show it to Steven, and then see where she comes down on the decision. "This place is not going anywhere. You have time to think about it for as long as needed. No hurry, no worry. Do you want to get out and look?"

Suzanna looked like a deer in headlights but nodded. That was step one.

They got out of the car and went to the front door and Donna used two keys to open it. The foyer was beautiful with a large glass chandelier and large entrances to different parts of the house on the right and the left but a beautiful white spiral staircase that led upstairs.

Chapter 17

They went up the staircase with a simple oak banister with white spindles that matched the stairs. There were five bedrooms upstairs, each with their own private baths. Three bedrooms on the left of the staircase and two on the right. One of which was the primary suite which was grand enough for a queen. The bathroom was larger than her apartment back home and each room was beautifully and individually decorated. She was totally in awe of the primary suite. It was as if it was decorated just for her. She hated to admit it, but she loved it. Loved all of it. Was charmed by it and she had barely touched the surface of all it had to offer.

Downstairs had two more bathrooms for guests, a small ballroom, and a small white baby grand piano. A large dining room with a large table that sat twenty-four people and then a small intimate dining area with a solid oak dinner table and six oak chairs with white and gold accents on the seats. In the corner, beside two huge windows that went floor to ceiling, were two comfy chairs and a small, round table between them.

The kitchen was larger than a small house and it had French doors to the side of it that opened up to an intimate courtyard with several different areas to sit and read or just rest watching the clouds float by. Another door went out to the side with a large, heated pool that had panels that enclosed it in the winter so it could be heated. A small bathhouse was in the back with twenty-tree acres of beautiful, wooded landscapes and hiking trails. It was expertly landscaped, even the wooded area had pathways going two different directions. Only God knew what was to be experienced back there. Today she would only be able to guess. They had spent so much time looking that supper was going to be late. Her mind swam with all the details, and she wanted to share the house with Steven.

"What did you think, Suzanna? Donna asked. You really didn't say much."

"It is a bit overwhelming. I would feel like a princess living there. I actually love it, but I don't know what Steven will think." Suzanna said.

"I know it's a lot to digest. Baby steps, grasshopper. Talk it over with him, and you two need to go together and look at it. Donna said.

"Sure, one step at a time. I don't even know if I can afford it."

Donna laughed. "Oh, honey, you can afford it and much more."

They pulled in the driveway. Richard was home and had a few extra-large pizzas from and a giant salad from Vencenzo's for them all to share. It was very good, and they all ate too much, and retired to bed early. Suzanna fell asleep reading another book.

Chapter 18

Retiring early on a full stomach of pizza proved to not be a good idea. Four hours later, she woke up with heartburn and a mind that wouldn't shut off after such a busy day. Turning on her right side, she contemplated picking the book back up and trying to read herself back to sleep, but she easily fell into restless thoughts of the day. The lawyer, the bank, the mansion. She fell back into a restless asleep, but because her mind refused to shut down.

She woke with a start around eight in the morning, got dressed, and went downstairs to find a quiet house. Donna left her a note explaining that Richard left for work, and she had to do some Thanksgiving prom shopping but should be home soon. A bagel waited for her in the microwave. This was the first time she had been left alone since she had been in Omaha. It felt strange and different. She ate her bagel, then called her sister.

"Hi Deb, how is everything going in Kentucky?" Suzanna asked.

"You know that crazy neighbor we have up here? Well, she was outside naked and turned on the water hose and gave herself a good old-fashioned bath—soap and all. The police came and took her somewhere. Nobody knows where, but I didn't call them. I wanted to, but I felt sorry for her. She has no family. So how are things in Nebraska?" Deb asked.

Suzanna told her everything that had been going on, including getting the money, her relationship with Steven, their dates, the mansion, and her idea to stay in Omaha. She asked if Deb wanted to come for the holidays.

"That would be nice. I think I just might do that. Come up when the primary school takes off for the Christmas holidays and be back in time for the New Year," she thought out loud. "Hey kiddo, I am so happy for you. I can't wait to meet your new beau. I'd love to see your mansion. I can come for a few weeks in the summer, too. It'll feel like we are kids again."

"I am so glad you are okay with all of this. I was worried about how you would feel if I moved here." Suzanna shared her feelings of guilt and insecurity.

Deb answered, "Flights go back and forth every day, and one button on my phone and there you are. Quit worrying about everyone else, concentrate on what you want, and focus on your new, handsome pastor."

They sent their love, hugs, and kisses and hung up. Donna came through the door with her hands full of groceries and Mike's tuxedo for the prom.

Suzanna jumped up to help her carry everything to the dining room and kitchen.

"The prom is tonight. Are you still going with Steven as a chaperone?" Donna managed to say despite being breathless from carrying three bags of heavy groceries and walking up the stairs.

"Oh my, I forgot all about it!" Suzanna cried out.

"Don't worry about it. I have us both our own little prom dress still in the car. I'll get it in a second."

School let the kids out an hour early to get everything prepared and even Richard came home early from work. Donna did not have to cook supper because dinner was provided. It was top secret. Nobody, except the prom committee, knew what was going to be served and for once they kept it under wraps.

Mike was so excited when he and Richard, the handsome devil he was in a charcoal gray tuxedo left to go pick up Abigail and drive to the school. Not before Donna pinned a small blue carnation bud to his and Mikes left lapel.

Suzanna dazzled in her shimmery, silver, mermaid-style long, and slinky dress with long sleeves. Donna bought her matching heels and a matching handbag. She had a respectable, low neckline with a necklace that looked worth a million bucks. It wasn't.

CHAPTER 18

Donna was breathtaking in her long, navy dress with silver accents around the neck and long sleeves with a beautiful silver belt that showed off how trim and fit she was. With her dark hair pinned up and flowing tendrils around her face, it looked as though it took her hours to get ready.

"Are we ready?" Donna asked. She twirled Suzanna around, admiring how beautiful she was. "You look great, Suzanna."

"Are you sure my hair looks good put up this way?" Suzanna asked, unsure of the quick hairdo Donna seemed to be a master putting together at the last minute. She had curled tendrils down all to the right side and a big silver broach pinned to the left side with a few curls that flowed across her face.

"Are you kidding, my dear? You are beautiful." Donna encouraged.

"As are you, cuz," Suzanna replied.

They looked at each other and laughed before they walked out the door to go to the first prom either of them had been to in quite a few years.

Chapter 19

Suzanna felt like a young schoolgirl again as she and Donna walked into the elegantly decorated school gym. Richard and Steven were already there with a half a dozen other faculty and staff.

Suzanna and Steven's eyes met the minute she walked into the beautiful gym decorated with white shiny and sheer material that hung in the middle and draped to a real carousel ring of beautiful white horses that enclosed the dance floor with subdued crystal lighting. On the outside of the ring of horses were small round tables with candlelight and large tables of six to eight for those who preferred to socialize with friends. The room was already full of young people who were laughing and smiling into the eyes of their dates. Ahh, young love is grand. Mike and Abigail went over to them to say hi and complimented Donna and Suzanna on how great they looked.

"I would have to agree," Richard said as he gave Donna a peck or two on the cheek before handing her a corsage of blue carnations.

"You look exceptionally handsome yourself, husband," Donna replied.

"Mom, Dad, not here!" Mike scolded. He and Abigail walked away holding hands.

"The most stunning female in the room," Steven complimented Suzanna as he walked up behind her and gave her a long peck on her neck, which gave her chills and filled her with an intensity of love she had never experienced.

"Thank you, kind sir," she replied. She turned around to face him. He had a silver and white rose corsage and began to gracefully pin it to her dress. "You look most amazing yourself."

Chapter 19

"Would you like to dance?" He asked.

"Should we? I mean we are chaperones," she responded.

"No one is going to notice or miss us." Steven joked. He took her hand and gracefully led her to the dance floor and as he gracefully led her across the softly lit room she melted in his arms. One could not determine who was who as they danced as one.

The evening went by way too fast, and it appeared everyone had a good evening as they stood by the door to tell the young people to be safe going home.

Steven took Suzanna home with a short detour—dinner at Waffle House.

"What would you like?" Steven asked.

"Just something to drink—a Coke or something. I'm not hungry in the least little bit."

He laughed and he ordered a platter of biscuits, bacon, eggs and gravy.

Suzanna sat and watched him eat as she talked to him about the house Donna showed her.

"Would you like to see it?" She asked.

"No, I have been in it plenty of times. The couple who lived there was part of my congregation."

"I'm confused. I thought she married in Paris and named her daughter Paris."

"Yes, that's true, but her husband died before she moved and then she remarried." Steven answered. "What do you think of the place?"

Suzanna thought a moment before answering. "I liked it well enough, I guess. I just can't see myself living there. I know I can afford it, but do I want to live that extravagantly? I am just not sure."

"I understand how it would give you that impression at first, but if you go and see it a couple more times you will realize it is not as elaborate as your first impression gives you," Steven offered. "I'll go with you if you would like me to. I would have no problem living there in case you were wondering. It is close enough to church and would give us security," Steven offered.

"Are you thinking about moving in?" Suzanna teased.

"Quite possibly—depends on a few things," he said, then stuffed a mouth full of biscuit topped with gravy.

"Depends on what?" She asked.

He gave her a shy grin and continued eating. He never took his eyes off her. He never wanted to forget how beautiful she was. "You know you look like a princess, don't you?" He asked.

"Then you, kind sir, are my Prince Charming," she answered. Then she pulled out her phone and took a picture of his mouth full of biscuits and gravy.

As Steven pulled up in front of Donna and Richard's house, they sat there a couple of minutes before he took her hand gently in his and raised it to his lips and kissed each finger passionately. "Suzie Q I find it difficult to understand my feelings for you. My wife died a painful death from cancer and the memory of that is still fresh in my mind. However, the minute our eyes met I knew you were brought here by God. That I would fall in love with you. Sometimes love is like a lightning storm and other times like a pot of water boiling on the stove. You have to wait till you see if the water gets hot."

Suzanna laughed. "Does that come from scripture?"

"No, quite contrary. It came from my great-grandad who passed it on to my grandfather who passed it on to my dad who married his lightning," he answered.

"We have never talked about your family. Are they still living? Do you have any brothers or sisters?" She asked.

"My folks are still living, and I have one sister. She is married and has two children. And I have a brother who is married and has three boys. They all live in Lincoln, Nebraska, and all still go to the church my great-grandpa founded. I am the only one who followed in his footsteps by joining the ministry. At least paid ministry. We are all ministers in one capacity or another, are we not? We don't all get paid a salary for it—just a blessing and a reward in heaven."

"Yes, that is true indeed. My grandfather was a minister before he died. Most all of my family is gone now except my sister, Deb. She will be coming

Chapter 19

for Christmas while school is on break. She is a schoolteacher," she added. "I have truly enjoyed this evening. All of it. I felt like a princess and have enjoyed just being out here with you." She blushed.

"You are a princess, and I have enjoyed tonight more than you know. Will you be coming to church in the morning?" He asked.

"Certainly," she confirmed.

He stepped out of the car to open her door and walk her up the steps. As they got to the door, he turned her around and wrapped her in his arms and held her as his lips gently touched hers and the passionate kiss melted her heart, and she wanted this moment to last forever. As he whispered in her ear, "Goodnight, Suzie Q." Steven turned to leave with her standing there wishing that moment could last forever.

Chapter 20

Once again, it was difficult for Suzanna to sleep. Her mind would not shut off. All she could do was think of every amazing and wonderful part of her magical evening. How she had felt like a Princess in Steven's arms. She thought about how beautifully the prom committee had decorated the gym and transformed it into such a magical place for dreams to come true.

Donna left the small foyer table lamp on, so she could safely find her way up the stairs. She took her heels off and crept quietly up the stairs and into her little sanctuary. Once under her comfy covers and fluffy pillows, she had hoped sleep would come quickly with as tired as she was. Unfortunately, that did not happen, and her mind jumped from feelings of being blessed and fighting to shut her mind off so she could get some sleep.

As she got ready for church, Donna popped her head in to see if she was up and was going to ride to church with them or drive herself.

"I think I'll drive this morning. I don't think my Pathfinder has been out of the driveway since I got here," Suzanna answered. "Do you think you could help me with this zipper?" She chose a red, wool dress with large lapels at her neckline and a thin black belt that gave her outfit the appearance of a two-piece set. Simple stud, pearl earrings completed the outfit along with short, red heels and a matching red clutch in lieu of a purse.

"You look stunning, as usual," Donna complimented her as she zipped the back of the dress. "How do you think last night went?"

Suzanna gave a big grin. "Magical. I felt like a princess."

Chapter 20

Donna smiled. "I heard quite a few compliments about how beautiful you and Steven danced. It was as if you had practiced together for months."

"I really enjoy dancing with him. I feel safe and complete when I am with Steven," Suzanna replied, blushing from sharing a confidence.

"You are good for each other. It makes us all so happy for the both of you," Donna replied. "We are about to leave. Do you want us to save you a seat in our usual spot?"

"Yes, of course. I'll be right behind you. You didn't leave me a bagel in the microwave by any chance, did you?"

"What do you think?" Donna looked back at her and gave a wink as she walked out the door. "Be careful, Buttercup."

The main parking and overflow lots were full. She was glad Donna saved her a seat.

It took her some time to find a place to park her Pathfinder, but she found a spot pretty close to the door and walked in just as the worship service began. They had a large choir that wore red robes, and they sang a song she wasn't familiar with, but the words were on two giant screens on each side of the choir.

The words to "He Touched Me" reverberated through the sanctuary as the keyboard, drums, and guitar played the music. She found Donna, Richard, and Mike right where they were supposed to be and sat down beside them. She looked to find Steven. He sat alone in a chair in the front on the left side of the sanctuary. He looked so alone, but she knew he was never alone. His one true God was His constant companion. His faith in God was one of the most enduring things about him. His faith never wavered. It remained strong and true. She realized at that moment how much she really loved him. She took her mind off Steven and focused on the Savior, her almighty, Creator, her heavenly Father and the Holy Spirit.

How great thou art and Amazing Grace a communion meditation and communion and then Stephen stood up to go to the gold metal podium to speak.

Steven thanked everyone for their faithfulness by being there and announced a meeting to discuss the church's Thanksgiving dinner scheduled for the Saturday before Thanksgiving. It would be on Monday evening in the sanctuary promptly at seven.

"Let us begin with a moment of silence before we pray," Steven said. "Father in Heaven, we ask that you be with us this morning and bring us joy in serving you and peace by living your word. We pray for healing, provision, and forgiveness. We thank you and praise you for all your blessings. We praise you for all you have done, for all you are doing, and for all you are about to do. Because you first loved us, we love you in return, and we seek your blessings in our lives. And everybody says, amen." Thank you. You may all be seated.

"Roman 10:13 states, 'Everyone who calls on the name of the Lord will be saved. Names are very important to people. If nobody knew my name, they may not know who I am. My name is written on my college degree and my high school diploma. If I was married, it would be on my marriage certificate. It's on my birth certificate and my paycheck. There are names that pertain to my occupation. You may be a plumber, construction worker, Pastor, lawyer, Doctor. God's name is a revelation of who He is. *Jehovah Rapha* means a God who heals. *Jehovah Shalom* is God our peace. *Jehovah Jireh* is the God who provides. Jesus is our Savior. There are several others, but you know what I am trying to explain. We are moms, dads, sisters, and brothers. Those are aspects of who we are to certain people. We need to praise God and use the names for which we praise him for. And lift up thanks for all of who we are to him and all of who He is to us. God likes it when we call him by name, and He enjoys hearing our praises.

"Finally, Jeremiah 10:6 states, 'There is none like you, O Lord; You are great, and Your name is great in might.' John 14 states, 'If you ask anything in My name, I will do it.'

"Do you have any mountains that need to be climbed this morning? If there is anything you need special prayer for, please come forward and our prayer partners will pray with you and/or for you. Whatever your need, we will stand with you in agreement as we sing our closing hymn 'Trusting Jesus.'

"If you wish to participate in Communion, the plates are in the back of the room and an Elder is beside each plate to pray with you or for you when

Chapter 20

you receive it. God bless you this Lord's day. Stay safe and stop in the back to say hello as you leave this morning."

Steven stepped down from the podium and walked over to Suzanna. She smiled up at him during the whole sermon. He held out his hand to her and she took it. He raised his arm for her to stand and walk with him to the back of the church. As he greeted people, he introduced her simple as Suzanna who was visiting from Kentucky and was Donna Wilcox cousin. Everyone was pleasant and gave all-knowing smiles.

The biggest smile was from Steven himself. He had grown to be happy again. Very, very happy.

Chapter 21

Lincoln, Nebraska, the state's capital was a much bigger city than Omaha, but Steven's parents lived on a six-hundred-acre farm that was thirty miles outside the city. Their big, beautiful farmhouse had been restored and remodeled several times and reminded Suzanna of an old, southern plantation home instead of an old, country farmhouse. With a large wrap around porch, a few swings, and a large white table with white wicker chairs, it already felt warm and welcoming. A large quilt lay across one of the swings and Americana pillows were tossed in nearly every chair. There was a large rocker on both sides of the front entry double doors. Those doors led into a sunroom which had a fireplace and a large, family portrait above the stone mantle.

Steven had wanted Suzanna to meet his parents for Thanksgiving, so they planned to stay a few nights with them.

Steven knocked quietly on the front door, but his mother was already there and opened it to give warm, loving hugs to Steven and Suzanna. His father was just a step or two behind her to welcome them both with a lot of sincere love. It didn't take Suzanna long to see Steven's family was close and loving, and they instantly made her feel part of it. Julie, Steven's mother, had long, gray hair piled in a bun on the top of her head. She wore a beautiful blue and yellow checkered apron over a solid navy blue short sleeved dress with a white collar and hung modestly just below the knees. Around the white collar hung a simple silver cross necklace. Steven's dad, Bill, had a nicely trimmed gray beard and short salt and pepper hair and wore dark blue jeans and a long sleeve blue checked shirt which was rolled up to the

Chapter 21

elbows and they both wore very happy smiling faces. Suzanna instantly felt at ease and at home. As they greeted each other, Suzanna heard a few sharp, excited barks and turned around to see a young, happy, Sheltie puppy who wagged her tail to get in on all the greeting.

Suzanna said, "Hi, Millie, you need some hugs too, don't you girlfriend?" They all laughed and Julie invited them into the family room to visit a while before dinner. The rest of the family arrived a short time later. All of them brought goodies for the Thanksgiving feast. Introductions were made, and Suzanna hoped she remembered everyone's names and who belonged to who. She never asked, but it was obvious Steven was the youngest in the crew of three children. His sister, Jennifer, was a very attractive blonde. And her two children, eight and ten years old, had already run upstairs to play with their cousins Michaels 2 boys, age 8 and 9. The two-year-old stayed with Michael's wife, Carrie Ann.

The farmhouse table was big enough for the whole family to sit together and a side table was dubbed the children's table and sat beside the big adult table. The buffet table in front of the big bay window was filled with deserts. Suzanna was partial to pumpkin pie at Thanksgiving, and she was not disappointed. Steven's Dad asked Steven to say grace. They all grew quiet and Steven blessed the meal. Even the children were polite and bowed their heads. Then the festive holiday conversation became a bit more muted. Suzanna wasn't good with large crowds of people she didn't know well, and she wondered how Donna and her family were doing. By now, other members of the family knew about her arrival in Omaha, but she hadn't seen any of them. Everybody's lives were so busy that visiting with family got pushed to the back of the list of things to do. Donna assured Suzanna they would all get together for Christmas, but she really wasn't that concerned. Steven was the only person she thought about these days.

After polite conversation at the table, they retired to the sunroom and Julie asked Suzanna about her future plans.

"I will be here until the first of the year for sure. After that, I am not quite sure, but I am looking for a home close to my cousin and the church,"

Suzanna replied. "I would like to do some charity work or something else. I am not going to worry about work until after the first of the year."

Michael, Steven's brother, asked, "How long will your company in Kentucky allow you to stay? Are you on vacation?"

Suzanna looked toward Steven and hesitated before responding, "I am on temporary leave until I decide. Under the circumstances they have given me a lot of flexibility."

Bill spoke up and asked about the circumstances.

Steven chimed in. "Suzanna was born in Omaha, but when her grandmother passed away her family moved to Kentucky. Her brother recently found their mother's will, which made her the beneficiary of her grandfather's estate. So, she has been in Omaha to get it settled since he died in a hospital in Omaha."

"I have been staying with my cousin and her family. They are members of Steven's church," Suzanna added. "It has been great reconnecting with them and reliving childhood memories."

The baby had been asleep in Carrie Ann's arms but woke up fussy. "I think this little one is ready for his own bed. We might think about heading down the road."

"I think so, too," Michael agreed. "I have to go into work for half a day tomorrow." Michael stood and called out to their other two boys. They ran down the stairs and grabbed their coats while chasing each other out the door.

"It's been nice meeting you Suzanna. Don't be a stranger. Come and visit anytime. You don't even have to bring Steven."

Everybody laughed and agreed.

It wasn't long before they were all settled down for the night. It had been a long, busy day for everyone, so they retired early.

Steven had his own room and Suzanna slept in his sister's old room, which still had baby dolls, an old crib, pink curtains, and a chenille bedspread. The room was warm and there was a King James Version Bible on the nightstand and a small lamp to read by. No television or radio. Just the basics of comfortable country living. She was surprised how quickly she fell asleep and stayed asleep.

The smell of bacon drifted up the stairs, waking her.

Chapter 22

Suzanna could not believe it was already Saturday morning. As she packed to head back to Omaha, she reflected on the previous day. She and Steven had a wonderful, relaxing visit with his folks. Even a short horseback ride through a beautiful meadow with a picnic lunch could not have gone any better. The weather cooperated with them as they allowed the horses to lead them to familiar places before they found an old hay barn that hadn't been used in a century or two and had a spark of magic. They used a couple of hay bales to set their food on and Steven brought a quilt for them to sit on. The horses, Midnight, named for obvious reason was Steven's horse, and Winnie—a beautiful Appaloosa—walked around the barn picking at the scattered hay. They ate turkey sandwiches on hamburger buns and had small handfuls of chips. Steven brought a surprise for Suzanna by bringing a piece for both of them of His Moms homemade, special recipe pumpkin pie.

Steven handed Suzanna her sandwich on a small paper plate along with the scattered chips he brought his lips to hers and gave her a gentle peck. "Bon appetite," he whispered in her ear and followed the first kiss with a second more passionate kiss along her neck just under her ear. She smiled as she reciprocated by cupping her hands along his cheeks and resting on his chin bone and kissed him long and hard on his soft lips which brought them together melting in each other's embrace for a couple of minutes. As they broke apart Suzanna told Steven, "I can't remember the last time I have enjoyed myself this much. The last few days have made me feel so blessed. I almost hate to leave tomorrow. Your parents are amazing. So warm and loving."

"I know one thing," he responded. "They think the same about you Suzie Q. My mom already thinks of you as a daughter."

"She is a very sweet lady. You have been blessed beyond measure."

"Yes, you are right about that. Mom packed the pumpkin pie because she remembered how much you liked it."

"Liked it? That's putting it mildly. It melted in my mouth," Suzanna said. Winnie nuzzled her face into Suzanna's armpit, trying to raise her arm for attention. She was a sweet and older horse and was obviously searching for an apple. Steven did not come unprepared. When Midnight saw Winnie get rewarded for her behavior, he decided to give it a try and after a couple of apples each Steven thought it might be time to head back to the house. As they packed up their things, Suzanna laid her hand on Steven's. "Thank you, Steven, for an amazing afternoon. I hope you have enjoyed it as much as I have."

"Actually, I think Midnight and Winnie had more fun than both of us," Steven laughed as Midnight toppled him over while looking for another apple.

They got back to the farmhouse before dusk, and the temperature dropped just as a dusting of snow fell. It reminded them both that winter was close. It was indeed time to head back to Omaha.

Chapter 23

Steven and Suzanna were quiet on their way back to Omaha. Both lost in their own thoughts. Suzanna drifted in and out of sleep until they reached the outskirts of town.

"I was wondering if you would like to go look at the Harrison House with me sometimes today. I know you will be busy fine-tuning your sermon this afternoon, but Donna called and told me there was someone else interested. So the Harrisons let her know we have first dibs, but it's time to make a decision." Suzanna said. "I know I have said it before, but I have enjoyed myself more than I thought possible. So, in case I forget, I want to thank you from the bottom of my heart. I haven't had such a great Thanksgiving in a long time."

"I haven't either Sunshine, and thanks are not needed. Is around 5:30 okay and then we can eat supper somewhere?" Steven said as he finished with, "Most likely at Donna's dining room. Do you really think she will not expect us for supper tonight after being gone during the holiday."

"I was thinking the same thing and 5:30 would be great." She replied as she looked up into the eyes that melted her heart. She didn't realize they had pulled up in front of Donnas' house.

Chapter 24

Donna was so happy to see them she was almost giddy. They were met with warm embraces from Donna, Richard, and Mike. After a short visit, Steven said his goodbyes. God called him to his study.

"See you around 5:30. Dress warm. There is a real chill in the air today."

Donna spoke up. "You guys want to have supper with us tonight? We have plenty of leftovers."

Suzanna and Steven looked at each other and laughed as they both said in unison, "Thought you would never ask."

Suzanna walked Steven to the front door, and they held each other for a quick second but the passionate kiss that followed showed Donna their relationship had definitely become closer and a bit more intimate. She was so happy to see the two of them together.

When Steven pulled into his driveway, he sat there a minute before getting out of his car. He felt so lonely when he came home. Home to him was not a place but a person, and Suzanna was his person. He didn't like missing her so much. She completed him. "I am going to ask her to marry me—and soon," he thought to himself. He was confident that he was in love with her and just as confident she was in love with him. He had to concentrate and finish his sermon. Tomorrow was the day he was to go to the Omaha Helping Hands Rehab and Nursing Facility to visit and serve communion to anyone that wanted him to serve it.

Steven went straight to his office and finished his sermon in no time at all, then he went over it again.

Chapter 24

Right on time, Steven picked up Suzanna so they could look at the Harrison House together.

As they walked out the door, hand in hand, Donna reminded them supper would be at 6:30.

The short drive over was filled with anticipation as this could be their first home together as husband and wife.

Suzanna showed more enthusiasm this time as she was more at ease discovering and visualizing herself with Steven as her husband but was jumping ahead of herself because even though he has hinted he hadn't officially proposed to her yet.

'What do you think?" She asked.

"It's a beautiful home, no question about it. I think you would be completely happy here if you didn't care about spending this much money. And I love all the right things about it with not one flaw I could see wrong. But the question is, how do you feel about it?" Steven asked.

"It is a beautiful home, but I don't quite understand why my heart or spirit doesn't jump out and say, 'this is it!'" She answered. "Does that make any sense at all because I am not sure it does to me?"

"It absolutely makes sense to me. I think where we live is an important decision and every house or home, if we are receptive to our inner spirit, will let us know if it is a god fit for us. I believe it is God's way of leading us on the path he has designed for our lives," Steven said. "I was hoping you might feel this way because even though it is a beautiful home, I don't feel the connection either. I have a friend in real-estate who just contacted me about a home that has just come up for sale and wondered if anyone in the congregation needed such a beautiful home close to the church. I mentioned you and has given me the code to get in if you are interested?"

"Yes, do we have time?" Suzanna answered.

"Absolutely! Let's go."

The house was around the corner from the church. It was hidden from the road and had a long driveway lined with large oak trees. It had stone pillars as you entered the courtyard to the house that sat on five acres. The house was warm and welcoming. The driveway took them to the back of the house with a three-car, detached garage. It had plenty of parking on the concrete driveway. As they exited the car, they both were amazed at the beautiful landscaping. A courtyard with a rolling stream that ran into a sizable Koi pond with several of them swimming toward them as they crossed the stream from over a beautiful wooden bridge and onto a large, landscaped concrete patio. The opposite side of the large, covered patio was a pool. Steven unlocked the door where they entered a sunroom, much like the Harrison house, but the similarities ended there. The sizable kitchen was warm and welcoming and there was a vaulted ceiling in the living room. You could see into the living room from the kitchen. There was three bedrooms upstairs and one bedroom down a short hall that led to a small, intimate family room with a beautiful brick fireplace and a huge television above it. Everything about the home was warm and inviting and the price was half that of the Harrison Home.

Steven could tell from Suzanna's demeanor that the house was by far a better fit for her, and he was quite pleased with it, but he would follow her anywhere.

"You really like this house, don't you?" Steven asked.

"I love it. How did you know? She asked.

"I just knew," he answered.

"What do you think about it?" she asked.

"I think it's perfect. As long as you're happy, I'm happy."

"I am more than happy! I am elated." Suzanna hugged him as he bent down to give her a long passionate kiss. His embrace always made her feel safe. She never wanted to be apart from him.

"We need to be heading to Donna's," he said as they broke from their embrace.

"Yes, just in time, too. I'm getting hungry." As she looked up into his warm beautiful eyes, he bent down into her soft, warm lips and their embrace seemed magical and electrical when he raised his lips from hers. "Will you marry me?"

She didn't hesitate for a second. "Yes, I love you Steven Landry." A tear dropped from her eyes and he kissed her check, down her neck, and melted

Chapter 24

into her soft lips where he lingered as tears weld up in his eyes, too. They broke apart and she used her scarf to wipe away his tears.

As they left the house, they were both so full of emotion they couldn't speak until they pulled into Donna's driveway and touched each other's hands and smiled before getting out of the car and walking up the steps. They knocked on the door and Mike happily greeted them.

Chapter 25

"You guys are fifteen minutes late," Donna chided them as she gave hugs. "I'll forgive you though. We have missed you guys—both of you." She gave them both a second hug. "Come on in and sit down, we are all starving, and it's ready and hot."

Richard shook Steven's hand and a gave him big pat on his shoulder as they took their usual seats.

"We played Monopoly on Thanksgiving Day, and I beat everybody. It was sweet!" Mike said, bubbling over with excitement.

Steven gave Mike a high five. "You might become a realtor or a banker someday."

"I already know what I am going to be," Mike answered.

"Oh really, what is that?" Steven asked.

"A famous basketball player, maybe even a coach. I like telling people what to do."

They all laughed and Richard asked Steven to say the blessing.

After they passed the food around and started to eat, the chit chat got everyone caught up from the last few days of being apart.

"Mike, guess what I did over the weekend," Suzanna said. Steven jumped in to stop her by touching her hand. She looked at him with a grin. "I rode a horse in a field and had an amazing picnic in a barn."

"Wow, that sounds great!" Mike said. "Maybe I can go to your parents farm someday, Steven."

Chapter 25

Steven began breathing again as he realized Suzanna wasn't about to say anything about their engagement. It was too late because Donna knew something was up and was not going to let it slide.

"Okay you two, what's up?" Donna looked from one to the other.

Suzanna and Steven looked at each other with warm smiles and nodded their heads in approval. They held each other's hand as Suzanna looked into Steven's eyes, as if to tell him it was okay.

Steven held up her hand and gave her a sweet kiss. "I asked Suzie Q to marry me and she accepted."

They all were so happy and congratulated them. "We would like to keep it quiet until we get our rings and make a public announcement," Steven added.

"We are just so happy for the two of you and feel honored you told us," Donna said. Richard nodded in agreement.

"Anyone want to play Monopoly?" Mike asked.

Everyone laughed and decided to humor him by saying yes. Three hours later, Mike won. But Richard told him he was tired and let him win. Steven had to quit because he had a sermon to preach in the morning and Suzanna was so tired she didn't pay a lot of attention. Donna was the final hold out, but he beat her fair and square.

Her final words were, "Don't get overconfident or you will lose next time. It will be a hard lesson because we often learn more from losing than winning."

"Not me" Mike bragged. He headed off to bed after giving his mom a hug goodnight.

When Suzanna's head hit the pillow, she was out. A couple of hours later she woke up and could not go back to sleep. She was so happy and overwhelmed. She couldn't believe she was so in love, had found a new home they both loved, and she was moving back to Omaha. She was sad to leave Kentucky. She grew up there. Her sister lived there. She was so young when she left Omaha. There were some vivid images of her childhood growing up, but not many. She somehow felt this was her destiny—her journey back home. She drifted back to sleep and woke with a start as Donna tried to wake her for church.

Chapter 26

It was a cold, cloudy, and windy morning. All four of them complained about the weather as they rode together to church in Donna's Suburban. Even on their short drive to church, no one could think of anything to say except to complain about the blustery weather. Richard was an Elder, so he stayed at the entrance door of the church to greet visitors and hand out prayer requests to members.

Mike, Donna, and Suzanna went to find their seats. As they spoke to many of their closest friends before soft music began. The service was beautiful, warm, and always thought provoking. Steven's sermon hit the heart with little arrows reminding everyone to be more loving and giving during the holiday season and the colder the weather the needier people will become. Share, Love, and Respect was the title of his message, and the congregation truly loved and respected their pastor.

Once all of them quit talking and were near the door, Steven came back to greet them. "Was wondering if any of you were up to having lunch in my meager home?" He asked.

They all looked at each other before saying "yes."

Suzanna rode with Steven.

As they pulled into his driveway, Steven parked his sports car and turned to his beautiful fiancé dressed in a beautiful orange/red ankle length dress and her go to simple pearl earrings and before the rest of the gang pulled up, gave her a long soft kiss that melted her heart and then said very softly, "I love you, Suzanna fair." S

Chapter 26

She looked into his eyes that were sparkling with tears, and with her soft, warm hands she held his cheeks. "I will love you forever and a day." Then she took a handkerchief and wiped his eyes clear of tears as he had wiped hers in the past. They hadn't noticed the big violet Suburban parked behind them until Mike pounded on the passenger.

"I'm hungry!" Mike said then laughed.

As Steven got out of the car, Mike opened Suzanna's door and they all walked into Steven's home. It was Suzanna's first time inside. It was a small gray-sided home with two bedrooms. Steven used one for his study where all the magic happened when he wrote his Sunday messages. The living room and dining room combo were good sized and painted a faint gray with white trim. A large picture of the Lord's Supper hung above the large, overstuffed gray couch which had a matching love seat and an enormous recliner that had a big floor lap and side table beside it. There was a worn Bible on the table with a pencil and journal beside it.

"Mike, you want to gather everyone's coats and lay them on the bed in the spare bedroom, please?" Steven asked and gave Mike a pat on the shoulder.

"Sure, Paster Steven. What's for lunch?" Mike answered.

"Well, how about tacos?" He asked.

"Really? You know that's my favorite!" Mike answered.

"I do! That's why I chose it. Hope everyone else agrees," Steven said.

"Of course they will. Do you need any help?" Mike asked.

"If you want to set the table. I have everything else covered. I started most of it before church. I just have to warm up some things, pull out the chips, get the salad out of the fridge, and we're ready."

Richard, Suzanna, and Donna were in a deep conversation about a member of the congregation that was in the last stages of breast cancer.

"She has a sweet four-year-old girl," Donna said. "She is worried about what will happen to her daughter after she dies. She has no living relatives. Her husband died in Afghanistan and his parents were already deceased and so are her parents. She has a sister who has five children of her own and cannot handle another."

Suzanna was terribly upset about this. "There must be something we can do as her Christian family."

Steven walked in just at the right moment. "There is," He said. He looked directly at Suzanna. "We can adopt her."

Suzanna looked into his deep, penetrating, blue eyes and knew he was serious. "I'd like to meet her first."

The seriousness was met by everyone with nervous laughter except Steven and Suzanna, who just continued to look into each other's eyes.

"Alright, how about Tuesday at the hospital. You can meet both of them and they can meet you."

"Are you speaking as a pastor or a fiancé?" Suzanna asked.

"Both," Steven answered. "I knew your heart would never allow a mom or child to suffer if you had the power to make the situation better. I would never suggest such a thing if I didn't feel in my spirit that you, me, and Mandie were meant to be a family. If you don't agree one hundred percent, I won't say a thing to try and change your mind. I know it's a lot to as.'" Steven took both her hands in his and whispered, "I love you." She whispered back and they kissed a small kiss of unity, not of passion.

Steven announced, "Let's eat."

Chapter 27

Sunday flew by, as it usually did. Church then lunch and chit chat with family and friends. By the time they started thinking about the time, it was late afternoon.

Lunch was awesome. "Now I know Steven can actually cook!" Suzanna joked.

"Oh yes, we have tasted his fine culinary skills before, Missy. He is an excellent cook." Donna praised. "You are getting a keeper, Suzie Q."

Suzanna glowed as she looked at Steven with a big smile as he was in a deep conversation about football with Richard.

Donna took the opportunity to bring up the little girl. "What do you really think about the chance of the two of you adopting that little girl?"

"I guess I trust Steven's judgement enough that I am open to it. I will reserve any opinion until I met them both. I love children, but I'm not exactly a spring chicken anymore but far from not wanting children of my own. We haven't even broached such a conversation beyond our feelings for each other. Marriages happen every day with man or woman beginning with a child from another marriage the only difference is this time it would be a child new to both of us." Suzanna answered as openly as she felt. "But if either of us has any reservations, I see it as a deal breaker for both of us unless we can resolve the issue together. Does that all make any sense to you? If so, what do you think?"

"Cuz, I have met the little angel myself, and her mom, and you are going to fall in love. That is just who you are, and I think you are a very special lady to do this for a dying woman whose biggest worry is who could take care of her child when she is gone," Donna answered.

The men grew quiet, and Steven smiled over at Suzanna. Richard smiled at Donna.

"What?" Donna asked.

"Nothing, dear," Richard responded. "Are you about ready to go home?"

"Whenever you are, my sweet," she answered, being silly and they all laughed.

"If it's alright, I'd like to bring Suzanna home later," Steven inquired.

"Absolutely, it'll be fine. Unless I am past curfew," Suzanna joked.

After they all left, they had some time to talk privately. "What do you think?" Steven asked. "I am so sorry for springing all that on you in front of everyone. It just kind of sprung out of me because I was planning to talk with you later."

Suzanna put her fingers to his lips. "*Shhh*, it's fine. I'm never afraid of speaking my peace in front of Donna. She understands me, she really does get me. So no worries. I meant every word I said, or I wouldn't have said it. I trust us and that we can be open about how we feel about anything. I just need to meet them both to reserve my final opinion, but I trust you and believe that is just a formality. So, we are good—better than good—we are great. So, are you going to kiss me yet or what?"

Steven looked into her beautiful eyes and with the palm of his soft, warm hand he felt her face. Caressed her forehead, then around her cheek down to her chin and brought her face close to his so they were intimately close and lips nearly touching before he kissed her chin then her cheek then her forehead, down to her nose and finally after looking closely into her eyes their lips melted into each other's as two becoming one and then h began to kiss her neck first one side then the other and back to her lips, soft, warm and caressingly before he stopped and said, "I need to marry you before I am tempted to make us both do something we will regret."

He pulled away and apologized.

"No apology needed. You didn't do anything wrong. You just need to make me an honest woman before we both get too carried away," Suzanna said. "Look at me."

His eyes had been averted.

"Could your guilt be coming from somewhere else?" She suggested.

He looked at her so sweet and intuitive and his heart melted. "You could be right. You are the first relationship since my wife died. I think I have been feeling guilty and I know I shouldn't feel this way. I think when we talk about possibly adopting a child it makes it somehow more real. Does that sound reasonable or make any sense to you? Please don't be offended or hurt," he offered.

"Oh, silly you could never offend me, and I deeply understand. Those feelings need to be addressed and faced so they don't become a sore that will fester. It is quite understandable for you to feel that way. I do understand, and I love you so much. I don't want you to suffer guilt, however misled or otherwise. Your pain is my pain."

Steven looked into her eyes and tears fell from his face and as she let the cleansing tears fall, she reached to hold his hand and he let out his pain that he had held onto for so long.

Chapter 28

Tuesday morning Steven picked Suzanna up to visit Melonie and Mandy. Her nickname was short for Amanda.

Suzanna was a bit nervous, but Steven was a lot more relaxed since their talk. When they got to the hospital, Steven needed a badge as a Pastor and I as his Pastoral intern. As they got in the elevator, he pushed floor five and they stepped back to allow others to get in and the elevator was nearly full by the time they reached their destination. He stopped at the nurse's station to get a follow up and Melonie was stable. That was the most they said. When we entered the room Mandy was sitting on her lap and they were playing some kind of children's card game.

Mandy jumped down. "Pastor Steven, Pastor Steven!" She leapt into his arms as he gave her a big, warm hug.

"Hi, little one what are you and momma doing this morning?"

"We are playing cards. Don't tell Mommy, but I am winning." Mandy shared excitedly and half whispered the winning part in his ear.

"Oh, I see." He said.

"Is this your friend you told me about?" Mandy asked.

"Yes, it is," he smiled at her.

"You are right, she is beautiful!" she said as she held out her hand and said "Hi I'm Mandy or sometimes Amanda, and sometimes depending on how good I have been behaving Amy Beth Marie Sorenson."

Chapter 28

Suzanna hand out her hand for a shake. "Well, it is nice to meet you Miss Amy Beth Sorenson. My name is Suzanna and, sometimes, depending on how good I am, I am called Suzie Q."

"I think I will just call you Suzanna. I think that is a pretty name," Mandy said.

"All of your names are beautiful just like you," Suzanna said.

The girl had long, thick, flowing blonde hair with a fine complexion and a few freckles. She wore a blue blouse with country overalls over top of the blouse and had beautiful, blue eyes and long eyelashes that were unusually a light brown. She was sweet and just as adorable as Steven said.

The little girl held her hand. "Come and meet my momma. She is very sick, but Pastor Steven has been praying for her and I believe God is going to make her well before Christmas. It is going to be a Christmas miracle."

Mandy walked her over to Melonie and let her hand go to jump in her momma's lap.

"Melonie, this is my fiancé, Suzanna," Steven said. "Suzanna this is Melonie. She is Mandy's Mother."

"Nice to meet you Suzanna, Pastor Steven is a keeper," Melonie said. "You better hold on tight to him. Mandy might steal his heart."

"I think it is too late for that." Suzanna laughed. "She is adorable. It's nice to meet you, too. How are you feeling today?"

"Not too bad. They haven't given me any chemo. Today so today is one of my good days."

"I'm so sorry you are going through this. Is there anything I can do?" Suzanna offered.

"At this point, there is little anyone can do for me."

"Well, I will keep you in my prayers—both of you." She smiled at Mandy.

"I don't need any prayers. I'm not sick," Mandy said. She tried to shuffle the cards in her tiny hands.

Before leaving, they all held hands and Steven said a prayer. He laid hands on Melonie's head.

After they turned over their badges, Steven was anxious to find out what Suzanna thought.

Chapter 29

"She is as adorable and precious and sweet as you described. She also thinks your prayers are going to bring her a Christmas miracle and her mother is going to be healed and go home." Suzanna told Steven when they sat in his car in Donna's driveway after being silent on the way home.

"I know she does, but it is more likely her mother may not make it till Christmas. If you are in agreement, we can have her set up the paperwork so when something happens, we will already be her legal guardians. What do you think?" Steven asked as he looked to her eyes for a hint of how she felt.

"I'd say she had better get the paperwork ready for us to sign. If you think it is the right thing to do, then I am fine with it. It's only the right thing to do if you are not going to give that girl her Christmas Miracle one way you had better find another way and I guess I am okay with being the second-best miracle for a little girl." Suzanna tried to make things not seem so dire. The situation could send her in foster care for the rest of her life and she knows that beautiful, innocent, little face was too sweet for that to happen.

"An instant family is a little scary, I will admit," Suzanna said, "but I don't need a job because I think God just gave me the best job a woman could have—being a mother to an orphaned angel. Unless, of course, God chooses to give her the miracle she wants."

Steven looked into her beautiful, soft, blue eyes to check for a hint of reservation, and he didn't see any obvious signs.

CHAPTER 29

She could tell he was struggling.

He wanted to be certain before any action was taken that she would have no hint of regret.

"No regrets, our decision is made," Suzanna said. "No turning back. It is going to be a blessing from heaven. Just as all children are. That's exactly how I look at it. Period. Okay?"

"Okay," Steven answered.

Two days later they signed the paperwork then went to the airport to pick up Suzanna's Sister for Christmas. They had Mandy strapped in the back seat for her first outing with Pastor Steven and Suzanna.

As they waited for Debra's flight to come in, Suzanna was lost in thought. She remembered playing in their backyard as kids, and their cousins and how they went fishing a lot in the summer and spent their holidays together. They didn't do much of anything without the families doing it together. They went to the city to sit in Santa's lap and to pick out their trees together. Many happy childhood memories. She come out of her thoughts when Mandy jumped off Steven's lap and came over to her.

"Are you going to be my second mommy?"

"Do you want me too?" Suzanna asked.

"I don't really know you that well, but Pastor Steven says you are a special person with a heart of gold, and he loves you, so I will love you too if I get to know you. Does it hurt to have a heart of gold?"

"Sweetheart, yes it sometimes does when you love someone very, very, much. But it is worth it because loving someone as special as you, or your mommy, or Pastor Steven can cause you pain when the people you love are in pain."

Suzanna held Mandy's little hands in front of her and she could see her mind processing what she said, and she looked at Steven to see that he was listening, and he was.

"Do you think I might have a heart of gold too because when Mommy hurts it makes me hurt too? Is that like what you mean?" She asked.

"You know what? I think you probably do have a heart of gold, and yes baby doll that's exactly like what I mean."

Suddenly, she saw a familiar face walking toward them. Steven picked Mandy up as she jumped and squealed. Deb saw them and she picked up her pace. They reached each other and they gave each other a giant hug.

"Oh, it's so good to see you, Sis. I have been missing you," Suzanna said. "There is so much to share with you that the phone just doesn't work. You know me. I hate phones." Suzanna spoke so fast she didn't give her sister a chance to say anything.

"I know you have been here awhile, but I am quite certain not long enough for that," Debra said. She nodded at little Mandy. Not letting go of her sister. She had missed her so much. They were very close and talked everyday about everything.

"I haven't had time to explain, so I thought it best to wait till you got here," Susanna said as they walked over to Steven and Mandy. "Steven this is my sister Debra. Deb, this is my fiancé, Steven. And this is our charge for the day, Mandy." Suzanna whispered that she would explain more later.

Steven stood holding Mandy in his arms. "It's nice to finally meet you, Debra. Suzanna talks about you all the time and about the fun times you all had when you were kids growing up here. And this is little Mandy. Her mommy is sick in the hospital, so we offered to take her out for the day. Are you hungry? Mandy's favorite pizza parlor is right around the corner."

"Yes, I certainly could eat a good pizza. My favorite food source," Debra answered with a laugh.

CHAPTER 30

Debra rented a car so she could have some freedom to explore on her own or with Suzanna, so Steven took Mandy back to her mom after they had their fill of pizza. Suzanna took a large to go order home for Donna and her crew.

Mike was ready to pounce on the pizza as soon as Suzanna and Deb walked in the front door. Richard and Donna were there for hugs and introductions. They sat in the living room for a change. Abigail was over, but they were busy devouring the different varieties of pizza.

The adults laughed so hard tears ran down their cheeks as they talked about some of the silly andreckless things they did growing up.

"You know, I'm lucky to have made it past puberty," Donna said. She reached over and took hold of Richard's hand. "And blessed to have this man beside me as a lifelong partner to keep me out of trouble."

"Our mom was able to do that all on her own," Deb said. She laughed, and Suzanna agreed. "She definitely kept us out of trouble—most of the time."

"I'm sure you have had a long day, counting your flight here." Donna said to Deb. "Would you like me to show you to your room? It's downstairs, but you get the whole suite to yourself. It is quite nice and roomy."

"Sure, "Deb answered. "I'm quite tired. It was a long flight and before that I was at school getting my classroom ready for the new year."

"What grade do you teach? I don't remember Suzanna mentioning it," Donna said as they went down the carpeted steps. Each one of them were carrying one of her bags.

"I teach fourth grade in a rural part of Meade County, and I love it. I. love the kiddos, too. I have never had a bad class since I started teaching," Deb answered.

"So, you and Suzanna live in the same county? How long have you been teaching?" Donna asked. She opened the door to Deb's suite.

"I have been teaching five years, and yes Suzanna and I live close to each other and we are very close friends as well as sisters. We go to the same church and hang out as much as we can," Deb answered. "Whenever school allows that is."

"Wow, this is gorgeous! I need you to redecorate my apartment," Deb said. "You were not kidding when you said it was big! My whole apartment could fit in here, and your decorating skills are amazing. Oh, my goodness! You even gave me my own Christmas tree and a gift basket? Thank you so much. You shouldn't have gone out of your way like this. It does make me feel special though," Deb exclaimed.

"You're family. This was no trouble at all. We feel blessed that you and Suzanna are here," Donna responded as she gave Deb a big hug.

Deb responded with a few tears of joy as she hugged her back. "It feels good to reconnect with family. We are isolated from family living in Kentucky. Our little brother and his family live in Lexington, so we see them only for holidays, weddings, funerals, etc., and an occasional cookout. With Mom and Dad both gone we never connected much with Dad's family, so Suzanna and I are close and then our church family is very important to us."

"Please make yourself at home. Your bathroom is behind door number one and a sitting room, reading room, or small living space is behind door number two and has windows and a door to a courtyard for relaxing. If you like our cold weather." Donna chuckled. "Feel free to come upstairs whenever you like. Suzanna's room is at the top of the stairs. Someone will make sure that whatever you are doing or wherever you are, someone will find you, so you won't miss any meals." They hugged again and Donna closed the door so Deb could get settled and get some rest.

As Donna closed the door, Deb turned around to admire her suite, which was decorated much like Suzanna's with a purple and pink flowered

Chapter 30

comforter and a picture of The Guardian Angel over the bed. A soft cream-colored angora blanket was spread across the bottom of the bed. Like Suzanna's bedroom, there were four, large, fluffy pillows that matched the colors of the comforter. The bed was king size with a plantation white, bedside table on each side of the bed and a softly lit lamp that hung down from the wall over the tables. There was a beautiful dresser on one side of the spacious room and a walk-in closet on the other side. She unpacked her things before there was a soft knock on her door. She recognized that knock and told Suzanna to come in. She had just sat down in a wing-backed chair that matched the bedspread. She was going to have to ask Donna if she bought it that way or if she made them. There was a matching chair on the other side of a small, round table that had a beautiful glass lamp with the guardian angel made of porcelain was built inside the wooden base of the lamp.

"How did you know it was me?" Suzanna asked as she walked into the room and sat down in the chair beside her.

"I would know your knock anywhere." Deb laughed.

Suzanna looked around. "Nice!"

They talked until the wee hours of the morning and they both decided to crash on the bed like when they were kids. They remembered so many silly things they did together. Before the crack of dawn, they were still laying there half talking and half asleep. Suzanna looked over at Deb. "I'm so glad you are here, Sis." That's the last words either of them remembered.

Chapter 31

The next few days flew by. Deb and Donna got to spend time getting to know each other and Steven and Suzanna spent more time with Mandy and often brought her to Donna's for family time. Mike adored Mandy and played games with her, although who knew how much she understood, but Mike didn't care. He was so good to her. Her and Deb became very close. Deb mothered her more than Suzanna did. They all loved her and treated her as one of the family. She enjoyed time away from the hospital, but often felt guilty being away from her mother who became frailer by the day. Mandy kept asking for Pastor Steven to pray for a miracle. She told him with all the innocence and love of a child of a God.

On Sunday, Suzanna rode to church with Deb so they had a few short minutes alone with each other.

"I can truly see why you love it here so much. You know home is where your heart is and it is no secret where your heart is, Sis," Debra said as soon as they got strapped into the car and headed out. She was always more independent than Suzanna even though Suzanna was the oldest. Debra had been all over Omaha in the few short days she had been there. She had a long visit with Melanie, went to visit her grandmother's grave, and visited with a few cousins that they will all get together on Christmas Eve in Donnas now very festive basement. Debra never played around with words either. She said what she thought, and she thought what she said.

"Is it that obvious?" Suzanna asked.

"Oh, my yes! And not to just your baby sister, but everyone who sees you together knows it. But it's not just that, Sis. It's something that reminds you or makes you feel you are home, and I am so happy for you." Deb answered and as they pulled into the church parking lot and put the rental car in park, she turned to face her sister and gave her a big hug. Both women smiled with a tear or two of happy tears. "There is something I want to talk to you and Steven about privately later, if we can squeeze in a few minutes alone."

"Of course, Sis. You want to move here, too?" Suzanna laughed as they got out of the car.

"A big resounding No. I love my life at home. I love teaching, I love Kentucky. You were older when we moved from here, so you have deeper and stronger memories here than I do. Kentucky is really my home." Deb answered as they walked up the church steps. They were greeted by John and Ellen Masterson, one of the Elders and his wife.

"Good morning, ladies," they both said.

"Good morning." The women replied as they exchanged hugs and handshakes and went to sit with Donna and crew as the choir began singing a song Suzanna was not familiar with but the big screen on each side of the choir had the beautiful words so they could follow. Suzanna fell in love with the music and after introductions and a couple announcements about the special candlelight service on Christmas Eve, the choir and a small group of children sang and played bells to *O' Holy Night*.

The service was quite beautiful, and Steven's sermon was on 1 Corinthians 13. Often referred to the love chapter. His sermon was so beautiful, the scripture was one of the first verses she ever memorized when she became a Christian and it was a long one. Even now, she knew it word for word. Lost in thought for a moment, Steven caught her attention when she heard him speak her name.

"Most of you know I am engaged to the mesmerizing young lady from Kentucky. Suzanna," Steven said. "Would you indulge me for just a moment and step up here with me, please? He had his mic pinned to his lapel, so when he walked away from the podium, he reached out his hand to help her up the two steps and held her hand. "If any of you have not met my Suzanna, she will be in the back with me after we adjourn."

"Suzanna, I asked you to marry me, and you said yes. Right?"

"Yes, of course." she softly answered.

Still holding her hand, Steven got on one knee and pulled out a square box and opened it.

"I wanted to make this official in front of all our Christian family and friends. Suzanna, will you accept this as a symbol of my love and devotion to you? To be a symbol of our engagement because I love you to the moon and back."

Suzanna looked into his amazing, beautiful eyes as he took the ring out of box and placed it on her finger. Her eyes filled with tears as she tried to get a closer look. He stood up and wrapped an arm around her as he walked them to the podium. "Would that be a yes, then?" He asked. Laughter broke out in the audience.

"Yes, yes, and a thousand times yes," she said directly into the podium mic. The congregation broke out in applause.

Chapter 32

They were all sitting around the living room laughing and having a good time after church when the conversation migrated to wedding plans.

"Let's get married on Christmas Eve," Steven suggested.

The women all spoke up and chimed in a big fat "No."

"Why not?" He asked.

"Several very good reasons," Donna said. "I think Christmas Eve and Christmas Day has their own set of traditions for everybody—not to mention church obligations."

"Yeah, you are right. I wasn't thinking."

"How about New Year's Eve?" Suzanna asked. "It's still this year and Deb will be here till the second of January. I would love it if my baby sister could be here."

They all chimed in "Yes," and so the date was set. When Donna asked them about the house, Steven said, "We have already put in motion the purchase of the house we went to look at on Merriman Lane. With so much going on, we haven't been able to take you over to see it. You either Deb. Why don't we all go over tomorrow afternoon?"

They were all in agreement. When wedding details started, the men followed Mike to the dining room table for his challenge to play Monopoly.

"I don't know why he is so obsessed with this game," Richard said. "It's ancient."

"Because I'm good at it," Mike said. "Besides that, Monopoly will never be too ancient. Abigail likes playing it. I even let her win occasionally."

"Well," Steven challenged, "Let's get it on."

The women in the living room took their discussion downstairs to the den and began making plans.

"Why don't we go shopping in the morning for a dress and things?" Donna suggested.

"Great idea!" Deb agreed. "It's not like Suzanna doesn't have any money to spend."

They all laughed. So much had happened in the short time Suzanna had been in Omaha that Suzanna's inheritance was seldom mentioned. She was very frugal with her money and didn't spend like an heiress.

"I know a great shop we can look for a dress. Andrea is the owner, a good friend of mine and a member of the church," Donna offered. "She also rents tuxedos."

"Yes, I think looking for her perfect dress is the best place to start," Deb agreed.

Suzanna intently listened and began to tear up. "I love you guys. You're the best."

They both hugged her as she sat on a big, old, orange, overstuffed couch. Donna on one side and Deb on the other. "Why are you crying sweetie?" Donna asked.

"I'm just so happy and so blessed, and I can't believe this Cinderella is really going to marry her Prince Charming with two good friends like you beside me. I'm just so happy." Suzanna sobbed louder and Deb and Donna cried with her as they too were so happy for her.

Richard poked his head down the stairs. "Are you guys alright?"

Donna, with a short tone of voice, which told Richard to mind his own business.

He didn't say another word until he sat down at the Monopoly table. He had his own problems. His son was going to beat him at Monopoly—again.

"Is everything okay down there?" Steven asked.

Mike answered in a voice that told Steven to not push it. "They told me to mind my own business. I might offer that's a good idea." Steven shrugged his shoulders and focused on the game at hand. He couldn't let this kid beat him—again. It was humiliating.

Downstairs, the girls got back to the business at hand and whole-heartedly glad they didn't have to play Monopoly.

Chapter 33

Donna and Suzanna sat around the dining room table the next morning drinking their usual cup of hot chocolate with marshmallows. "I got sidetracked last night and forgot to ask you where you got this Cinderella and Prince Charming thing you mentioned," Donna said.

Suzanna laughed. "When I was little, I constantly read those little fairytale books and my *Cinderella* was my favorite. Grandma would save Robbie and me all the little books that came into the Goodwill Store she managed and when we finished them, we would swap them out for the next batch that came in and the Little Golden Books, Momma just bought me so I could keep them, and I would read them over and over again. When things got rough, or when I got lonely after we first moved to Kentucky and I missed everyone here in Omaha, I would just imagine I was Cinderella and he would save me and take me to his kingdom and since he was a Prince, I would become a Princess and loved by everybody in his Kingdom.

"When I became a Christian, God shared with me that I was already a princess because I was a child of the one and only King of Kings and Lord of Lords. That revelation simply rocked my world and still does to know our God considers me one of His children. That anyone that accepts His Son as their Savior will one day go to God's home, our perfect home, Jesus, is preparing for us in heaven. I think that is such an amazing blessing that God loves His children so much that from Genesis to Revelation He did everything just so we can spend eternity with Him in heaven. God's amazing grace is truly amazing. How old were you when you were saved?" Suzanna asked.

CHAPTER 33

"I was saved when I turned twenty-one. Well, I was baptized on my twenty-first birthday. I know what you mean Suzie Q. I began to run around with some new not so good friends and got drunk one night. While driving home, some headlights were too bright for my eyes, and I drove off the road and hit a large tree head on. I was thankful I didn't hurt anyone, but I broke my arm and hip and couldn't walk for nearly six months. We had been going to church, but I hadn't taken it seriously until I saw how my new car was nearly split in two and the injuries I sustained were nothing of what they could have or should have been. Dad had already died, but Mom was so hurt and angry with me, but so thankful I was still alive that she said very little to me about the accident." Donna teared up a bit. "I was in rehab for a short time and that is where I met my Richard. He had a handicapped brother who was there for therapy for a while, and we just hit it off. We were young, but young love is so amazing, and it was his tenacity that led me to a real relationship with Jesus.

"A year later we were married. But before we got married, I was baptized, and his little brother died from his severe handicaps. We went through a lot together before we ever married. Spent a few years establishing our careers before thinking about children. After our first child I never went back to work. Steven has always been able to provide well for our family. It was after we moved here, we started going to the church we are at now. The first minister moved his family to Georgia.

"We have been so blessed by Steven's shepherding and his teachings and great knowledge of the word. He immediately filled in and the congregation loved him so much we all voted to appoint him as our full-time minister. We helped him through the tragic loss of his wife just two years after they started their ministry here. She has been a real loss, even to the church. Very devoted to children's ministry, and we to this day, we use some of the programs she developed before her illness and eventual death. Steven is a true testament of a child of God truly living a Christian life even when under such devastating hardships. We became fast friends and have always loved and respected him."

Donna, lost in thoughts of the past, looked down at her watch. "My goodness Cinderella, we need to get our buns up and get ready for our bride's day out with the ladies!"

Suzanna looked down at her watch and agreed. As she stood to her feet Donna put her hand on her arm and gave her a hug. "Thanks for sharing this morning. I am so blessed to have had you stay here with us. I hope after you guys get married, we can remain close."

Suzanna hugged her tight. "Are you kidding? You can't get rid of me that easily."

"Do you all know what time it is? Deb asked. "I am already dressed to go out the door to plan my big sister's wedding and you two are not even dressed."

Deb had climbed the steps and stood behind them laughing with her hands on her hips. "Do you have a bagel anywhere? I am starving."

They all laughed at each other and forty-five minutes later they were in Donna's Suburban turning out of her driveway and ready for their lady's day out and getting ready to enjoy seeing Suzanna spend some money. Weddings weren't cheap, especially for Cinderella wannabes.

Chapter 34

Much of what they needed, they were able to get at Donna's friend's shop called Wedding Dress and Things. When it says, "things" she really did have a lot of things and her friend Andrea was such a great help in guiding them each step of the way and explained what they needed and why they needed them. Suzanna's dress was the first and the most important item on the list. Most brides took weeks and hours to find the perfect dress; Suzanna already knew what she wanted and only had to try on five dresses before she picked out the perfect Cinderella dress.

Even though they teased her relentlessly, she didn't care. She knew what she wanted her dress to look like. She only had to decide between lace or tulle and long or short sleeves. The little particulars ended up with lots of tulle and lace with pearls and sequins everywhere. Very full around a tiny waistline and with no sleeves except what lay across her shoulder exposing a beautiful neckline that Steven is going to appreciate. They found her a stunning, sequined, layered necklace and matching earrings. With Andrea's help, Donna and Deb both chose their own dresses. They were both going to wear light red, but with different styles to complement their body types. Andrea offered to do Suzanna's hair and makeup on her wedding day. The tuxedos were ordered there as well. Suzanna picked out what everyone agreed would be perfect for Steven, Richard, and Mike but they would need to come and get actual sizing in no more than a couple of days.

"We haven't chosen a veil that will match the dress yet," Deb said.

"I don't want a veil; I want a tiara," Suzanna replied.

"I have the perfect tiara for a princess and a short veil that attaches to the sides and drapes in a half moon in the back and will not take anything away but only adds to the off the shoulder sleeves," Andrea said. "Come let me show you."

Andrea went right to the tiara. Suzanna thought it was perfect, and Deb and Donna were in total agreement.

"Andrea, your help has been so invaluable," Suzanna said. "I don't know how to thank you."

Andrea looked at Suzanna and Donna, and she gave Suzanna a hug as her tears filled her face.

"Oh, honey it has been my pleasure," Andrea said. "I feel honored you trusted me to help you with your dream wedding."

Donna mouthed " thank you" to Andrea who winked and smiled in return. Andrea suggested the best bakery for wedding cakes, the best florist for flowers, and the closest hot spot for lunch since they were all starving and tired.

All they had to do was pick a cake and the flowers, find a venue for the reception, and figure out who would officiate.

They lingered over lunch trying to tie up some loose ends and decided they may need a wedding planner if they couldn't find a venue at that late notice for New Year's Eve. After their minds were tortured over finalizing the plans they were pretty well spent for the day, and it was almost time to meet the guys at Merriman Lane to see the house Steven and Suzanna were buying. Richard and Mike were already there waiting and as they pulled in Steven pulled in behind them.

"I don't have to see another thing before I can tell this place was meant for the two of you and is a much better fit then the mansion I showed you," Donna said as the women exited the car. "It's charming, full of character, and looks homey and welcoming."

After they all went through the entire house from head to toe, and inside and out, Debra asked, "Why couldn't this be the venue for the reception? You would just need to find an unemployed wedding planner."

Chapter 34

"She's right!" Donna jumped on board immediately. "This place is perfect for the venue you guys. What do you guys think?"

They all agreed, so it was decided. It was a very productive day. They were all tired and hungry, so they ordered pizza and went home to crash and feed their hungry faces.

Chapter 36

They immediately began to help Donna fix supper as soon as they got home. Another long day was draining and of course all their thoughts were on Debra's revelation. Richard and Mike got home before Steven came in with good news from their realtor. "We can sign and close on our house tomorrow!" They all cheered their congratulations and Steven gave his fiancé a peck on the cheek.

As they sat down to eat supper, Mike offered to say grace. It was a beautiful, sincere prayer of thanks to their Lord. Donna and Richard beamed with love and pride.

"How did basketball practice go?" Donna asked.

"It was good," Mike replied. "We played a game against each other tonight to decide who will play in Thursday night's game."

"Well, did you get picked?" Donna asked impatiently.

As he shoveled a mouthful of his mom's homemade meatloaf, one of his favorite meals, he managed to say yes.

"He made two, three-pointers back-to-back in practice," Richard couldn't hold it in any longer, so he blurted out. "He was on fire this afternoon and coach was thrilled with his progress. He is becoming one of the top players."

Donna smiled with pride because Mike had struggled to stay on the team last year. This year, his improvement had been amazing. "That's awesome honey! Just don't turn into one of those obnoxious, rude, conceited jocks."

"Oh Mom, you know that will never happen," Mike said. "You've taught me better than that."

Chapter 36

They had a great relationship and that was important to Mike. He was quiet about it, but he knew how God expected him to treat others. He took the command Jesus told His followers to heart, "to love others as themselves." And that was Mike's desire. He hoped to follow in Pastor Steven's footsteps one day. He just kept it to himself.

Steven was aching to spend some time alone with Suzanna. "You want to drive over to the house and get some ideas on decorating and things?" He asked.

"Sure," She jumped at the chance, "but I need to help clean up first."

"No, you don't," Donna said. "Run along. We've got this. Go please, spend some time alone for a while. I'm sure you have things to talk about."

Suzanna knew exactly what she was referring to. The conversation with her sister was something she needed to share with Steven alone.

Deb spoke up to encourage her to go as well, although she really didn't need much encouragement and Mandy was busy trying to get Mike to play Monopoly with her which usually didn't take much encouragement. Spending time alone with Steven was something Suzanna longed for every minute they were apart.

She was quiet in the car ride over. It snowed the night before and there were large snowflakes falling on the windshield and there was already a fresh dusting of snow on the roads. They walked hand in hand into their soon-to-be home and once in the door Steven pulled Suzanna into him and gave her a long, warm, passionate kiss.

It felt so good to be in his arms. To feel that loved was overwhelming and Suzanna needed to break the mood.

"Sweetheart, we need to talk about something important. I just found out about it today."

"Does it have anything to do with Mandy?" Steven asked.

Suzanna looked into his beautiful, dark, blue eyes. It was as if he could look into her eyes and read her mind, heart, and soul all at once. "How did you know?"

"Honestly, it was quite obvious if you were paying attention, which I wasn't at first. Melonie told me."

"Told you what?" Suzanna inquired.

"She told me that Mandy wants Debra to be her new mommy. We had a long talk and prayed about it. Melonie is having the papers changed as we speak. Since Deb has been here, I noticed you stepped back a little as Mandy and Deb began to bond and develop a deeper relationship."

"But sweetheart, what do you think about it? I mean, how do you feel?" Suzanna asked. "I don't want to choose between your happiness and my sisters."

Steven smiled as he took her hand and felt the ring he placed on her finger. He brought it up to his lips and walked her to a small window seat in the kitchen and they sat down before he responded to her concern. "

"My love, you are not making a choice," Steven said. "Mandy, her mother, and Deb have made a decision and I couldn't be happier. I just didn't want that little girl to be placed in foster care. I love her and will miss her, but we will still be part of her life. I know your sister will give her a good home and so does Melonie.

"She is fine with her moving to Kentucky with Deb. They have spent quite a bit of time together and Melonie loves Deb, too. She just wanted us to be okay with her decision. Melonie even talked it over with her own sister. The sister still wants to be a part of Mandy's life and Deb already has her number and reassured her she will be up here visiting a lot with you moving here. Both of us, Melonie and I, are at peace with it. So, are you at peace with it?"

"I'm happy if everyone else is happy," Suzanna whispered into her love's right ear. "I can't wait until New Year's Eve."

"Me either," Steven replied as he placed his lips on her soft, moist, tender lips. "I can't wait until you're my bride."

"Soon, my love, very soon." Suzanna placed her lips on his soft neck and kissed him not once, not twice, but three times before he reached up with the palm of his hand and held her cheek and gently raised her head and as their eyes melded into one, they kissed more passionately than she ever thought possible and she believed it was because they loved each other so

Chapter 36

much. He then raised her hand to his lips and kissed each finger before lingering on the engagement ring and popped his head up.

"We need to go pick out our wedding rings tomorrow—after the closing of course."

She laughed merrily and wondered if they were ever going to get everything done before New Year's Eve. Christmas was closing in on them and they hadn't even bought a Christmas tree.

Chapter 37

Steven took Suzanna back to Donna's and walked her to the door. As she turned toward the door and reached for the doorknob, Steven touched her hand then held it and turned her around to wrap her in his arms.

She loved it when he did that. As she looked up, he planted his lips under her chin. "I can't wait until I don't have to drop you off anywhere except home with me," Steven whispered. Then he whispered how beautiful she was in her red dress that twirled when he turned her as it hung below her knees and her beautiful slender ankles seemed so delicate wearing those black high heels trimmed in red around the edges. His lips traveled to under her ear lobe and rested there and nibbled a teasing short nibble before moving back to her lips. He certainly knew how to make her want him in the worst way despite knowing he was forbidden fruit for two more weeks. She felt as though she were going to melt in his arms when they both heard laughter and Christmas music playing. They looked at each other and opened the door. They saw Richard and Donna dancing around the living room floor and Mike and Debra hanging tinsel on a big fir Christmas tree. The whole house smelled like Christmas and there were lit candles everywhere. The whole house had been turned into a living, breathing, magical, Christmas wonderland. It was beautiful. There was more fake snow in Donna's living room than there was real snow outside.

"What is going on in here?" Suzanna laughed.

Donna turned around in Richard's arms. "We are having a Christmas party. Come join us."

Chapter 37

They noticed Abigail was there. She and Mike were flirting.

Suzanna looked at Steven and he smiled down at her. They threw their coats on the couch and joined the party by dancing to *White Christmas*, which was Suzanna's favorite Christmas song. For more than an hour, they laughed, danced, and hung stockings on the mantle, not forgetting their last three additions to their family: Deb, Mandy, and Suzanna. Steven already had a stocking on their mantle. He had been family for a while now. They found homes for the last of the ornaments and Richard looked down and kissed his perfect bride goodnight. He couldn't keep up with the many years, but he could at least say he loved every minute of their married life. There was never a dull moment with Donna in it.

Steven kissed his angel goodnight once again at the door. This time he was inside, and he was the one opening the door to go. Suzanna pecked him on the cheek and whispered goodnight. He turned to remind her he would pick her up at 10:00 sharp in the morning. Their closing was at 10:30.

She closed the door and dreamingly rested her back against the door.

"You had a good night, I presume," Donna said.

"I did, and I have some amazing news," Suzanna said.

They all turned to her, expecting her to go on, but she held back. "You started decorating without me." Suzanna put on her fake pouting face with her lower lip hung low.

"You have a tree in the den, and we will help you with it tomorrow," Donna said, "but you have to choose the color of decorations and such silliness, and you have your own tree in your room to decorate any way you want to. Now, would you please tell us."

"Okay, okay." Suzanna smiled. "Deb you are going to be a mother very soon. Mandy and Melonie had been talking and Melonie realized how much Mandy loved you. And she knows how much you love Mandy. She asked the lawyer to change the paperwork. All you have to do is say yes and sign the documents."

Deb had already lowered herself onto the overstuffed couch.

"John Henry? Who's John Henry?" Donna couldn't help to ask.

Deb spoke up before Suzanna had an opportunity to speak. "John Henry signed the *Declaration of Independence*." She shrugged. "I think. Anyway, Suzanna is always doing and saying things that."

Donna looked at Suzanna first and then at Deb. "Well then, are we okay? If so, who wants a mug of hot chocolate before bedtime?"

The women couldn't get to the kitchen fast enough.

Suzanna rummaged around the kitchen. "Where are the marshmallows? Who's got the marshmallows?" She added a little louder. Suzanna saw Deb walk into the dining room carrying a big bag of soft, fresh, marshmallows swung over her shoulder with one hand and carrying her giant mug in the other.

"Sis, I love you!" Suzanna's voice was loud enough to carry to the dining room.

Deb turned around and grinned ear to ear.

Chapter 38

Steven, good as his word, was there to pick Suzanna up promptly at 9:55 in the morning. It took them ten minutes to get to the realtor's office and they waited for thirty more minutes before all the powers that be were there and ready for signing. Cash purchases were less difficult than mortgage loans and took a lot less time at closing.

They walked out owning a very big estate with a beautiful home that had lots of privacy. It was a home that would welcome family and friends with open arms.

They drove to Merriman Lane make some decisions about furniture. It snowed all morning and six inches built up on the roads, but the road crews handled it and the roads were not slick just wet. They hoped to have furniture before Christmas Eve so it could be situated for Andrea when she arrived to get things ready for the reception. Donna reserved a good friend of hers for photography.

"Seems like things are coming together." Suzanna let out a sigh of relief. "As long as we have the dining room, our bedroom, and the main living room ready before the wedding the rest can wait. Don't you think?"

Steven looked down at his phone. She had never seen that expression on his face before and was concerned. She placed her hand on his arm. "Sweetheart, is everything alright?"

He didn't answer or respond. He looked up at her beautiful blue eyes as he let a tear fall from his own.

"Honey," he said, "I have to go to the hospital. Melonie took a serious turn for the worse. They're not expecting her to make it. Do you want to go with me, or do you want me to drop you back off at Donna's?"

"I'm going with you. Someone needs to help with Mandy. Should I call Deb to come and be with her?"

"That might be a good idea," he said.

They were at the hospital in ten minutes and Deb arrived thirty minutes later. Donna stayed home and set up the church phone chain for prayers and support. She didn't need to make a parade of any more people than necessary.

Steven and Suzanna walked into her hospital room together and Mandy ran into Pastor Steven's arms. She was crying and then turned to hug Suzanna. Always thinking of the feelings of others even while going through such tragedy. "Pastor Steven, they said Mommy is getting worse will you pray for her to get better."

"Amy Beth Marie Sorinson, you remember what we talked about," Steven said. "God heals people in many ways. You know Mommy is in a lot of pain and is very, very sick, but in heaven she won't be sick anymore. There is no sickness and no pain whatsoever in heaven. Only happiness and joy. She will miss you, but she has found you Mommy Debra to help you grow up just the way your Mommy would have raised you. She loves you so much."

"But Pastor Steven, if she loves me so much, why won't she stay here with me?" Mandy sobbed.

Deb walked in the door and got down on her knees in front of Mandy. She had tears in her own eyes. "My sweet, sweet, Mandy. Your Mommy is needed in heaven. She doesn't want to leave you—not at all. But God is in charge, and he doesn't like to see His children in pain. He wants her to be able to fly with the angels. God knows everything, and He loves everyone, and He wants to wipe away your tears the way your Mommy does and the way I always will. Do you hear what God is telling you right now?"

"No," Mandy said as she looked around.

Chapter 38

"Sweetie, God lives in your heart and if you listen closely, He is sending you a message. Do you hear it?"

She shook her head and tried to listen closely as her sobs diminished.

"My dear, dear child. Do not be afraid. Be strong and courageous as David was when he killed the giant," Deb whispered to Mandy. "Do not fear because I will never leave you. I will always be with you because I am your God. You can talk to me whenever you want and I will listen and hear you. You are strong and I will always watch over you, and I will keep your mommy with me in heaven forever. She will never feel sickness or pain again."

"Did you hear Him, Mandy? Did you hear God speak to you?" Deb asked.

Her face lit up and she smiled. "I think so. Yes, yes I did." Mandy looked at Deb. "I love you Mommy Deb."

Steven stood at Melonie's bedside to pray over her and held her hand when she drew her last breath. Before she died, Melonie thanked Steven for taking care of her daughter. He told her it was a pleasure and a blessing to have gotten to know them both. Suzanna sat on the chair on the opposite side and heard everything from Melonie's bedside and Deb ministering to Mandy.

Mandy hugged and kissed her mother goodbye before Melonie closed her eyes, but she didn't shed anymore tears. Deb took her home to Donna's.

Deb never let little Mandy see her tears as they drove back to their home for a few weeks more. She tried to hear God's voice telling her not to be afraid, but to be courageous. God was always with her and would never leave her alone, ever. She got to know Melonie and thought of her as a friend. Melonie was a wonderful person and just from the short time they had known each other, Deb felt blessed to have known her.

Donna stayed up waiting for them to get home and offered Mandy some hot chocolate. Like all the women in the house, she loved hot chocolate and was excited to see such a big Christmas tree.

"Wow, I don't think I have ever seen such a big tree with all those decorations and look at all the presents. Has Santa come already."

"No, not yet. These are presents we give to each other," Donna said. "There are several under there for you too, Missy. But I think Mommy Deb is tired, so you both need to get to bed." Donna winked at Deb and Mandy gave her tiny little hand to Deb to hold as they walked downstairs. Mandy almost fell asleep before she hit the bed.

Chapter 39

Melonie had wanted to be cremated. She didn't want Mandy to have to look at her that way. They way everyone looked down into a coffin. A very small service at the Church with just family and a few close friends, a few close nurses and her doctor were there. Mandy didn't shed a tear. She told Pastor Steven that God told her to be brave.

Suzanna cried more tears than anyone though she tried to hide it. She had taken Mandy and Deb shopping for new clothes. She felt like splurging, and she always bought clothes when she was stressed. They had a good afternoon before the service, and they invited Melonie's sister over to Donna's, but she declined. They all told her if she needed anything, to let one of them know. She hugged them goodbye and they never saw her again. She didn't even say bye to Mandy. Obviously, there wasn't much of a relationship there even though she was her aunt. Deb did give her phone number and address.

That evening, they were all beat and retired early. The church had brought so much food Donna had to give much of it away.

"Do you feel like running over to the house for a bit?" Steven asked Suzanna.

"Sure, for a while—a short while."

On the drive over, Suzanna told him he did a good job at the funeral. He thanked her but little else was said. He was very quiet and sullen.

When they opened the door to the house, it was full of furniture in the dining room, living room, his study, and the more intimate family room. She looked at Steven then looked around and smiled. "It looks like home—a real home."

"Do you care that I went ahead and ordered everything without talking it over with you?" Steven asked. "We talked enough about what we both wanted, and we have looked at this very set that even matches in the family room but they assured me if you didn't like one thing or all of it, they would come and pick it up or exchange for whatever you wanted."

"Sweetheart, I love it. I love all of it. It is perfect. You know me so well. I don't know where you found the time but yes, it's okay. I love every inch of it."

"You get the pleasure of taking care of the bedroom. That's all your baby. The bedroom the sitting room and bathrooms. Are all yours my love." Steven said as he held her hand and brought it to his lips and gave her a kiss on the palm of her hand and then he reached her neck and kissed her moist beautiful pink lips and lingered there a while before he made himself pull away.

"One more week my love, just one more week." He held her face with the palms of both his hands and looked deep into her beautiful eyes. He smiled. "We will soon be together as husband and wife."

They held each other tightly and passionately as their lips caressed each other's until Steven knew if he didn't let go, he never would.

He took her hand in his and they walked out the door. Soon they will be home for good.

Chapter 40

Christmas Eve

Suzanna woke up early because she needed to be at the house for the bedroom furniture delivery. Modern distressed white headboard with a beautiful soft coral satin fabric with pleated buttons throughout, a massive mirrored dresser, a cedar chest, lots and lots of pillows, sheet sets for the king bed and a surprise for Steven. She took one of Donna's pictures she had taken of Suzanna and Steven and had it enlarged and framed in a beautiful distressed, white frame that matched the furniture. Their large walk-in closet could hold anything and everything they owned, but it was important to get the bedroom beautiful and perfect before their wedding night. A magical day and night. One she had always dreamed of. Marrying someone as special as Steven was truly a blessing from God, and she thanked him for it every day. A girl who dreamed for Prince Charming was blessed with something even better. Only God could have planned something so amazing and perfect for them both.

Donna wanted to go with Suzanna to the house and help her straighten up some. "Donna, I appreciate you coming so much, but you have so much to do to get ready for tonight." Suzanna told her. "But I am so glad you are here."

"Steven did such a good job picking out all of this without you," Donna commented on the living room, dining room, and den he surprised Suzanna with. Buying and delivering without telling her.

"I know, and he said he would send it all back if I didn't like any of it. But of course he already knew what I liked because we looked at it in a couple of local furniture stores. Comparing prices, warranties, styles et. So, he knew what my favorite and my style, and I was loved everything," Suzanna replied.

Two and a half hours later the bedroom furniture showed up. Donna and Suzanna made the bed and tossed pillows, in the bedroom and family room.

"All ready for love and fun one week from today," Donna commented.

Suzanna playfully half punched her on the shoulder. Donna looked down at her watch. "My goodness, It's almost time to take the turkeys out and put in the pheasant and the duck. Thank God for two ovens!"

"How many people are coming tonight?" Suzanna asked on their way home.

"Let's see, besides our own family, Steven's parents are coming then will go to Steven's for the night. You guys will have an intimate morning there before they head back to their farm. Then there is Uncle Dale's family. I'd say we'll get to thirty-five people."

"Really? That's a lot. Is there anything you need help with?" Suzanna asked.

"Of course not, silly. I love throwing dinner parties. This is just family. I've got this. No worries." Donna assured her.

The afternoon flew by with a flurry of activity. The cooking, the setting up the tables downstairs. The pies got baked early, thank goodness, because it took longer for the birds to cook then they thought. Even little Mandy pitched in like a little trooper and helped carry some of the light stuff down the stairs. She had been doing well since her mother's passing, but Deb was very protective of her and spent most of her time with her.

Richard pitched in the best he could around all the women. You could tell he was out of his element and mostly just did the heavy lifting and moved tables around. Donna brought out special Christmas China, so he was ordered to keep his hands off of those. He tended to be a klutz around delicate things.

Around five o'clock, they all took turns getting dressed for the big party. Suzanna was the first because Donna suspected Steven would be early with his parents. She was right. Mike entertained them in the living room until

Chapter 40

Suzanna came down from her bedroom. Steven's eyes were aglow as he saw his beautiful bride-to-be.

"You look amazing, my love." He whispered in her ear.

"Thank you, my dear. You look smashing yourself," she whispered into his ear. Then she greeted Stevens parents with hugs.

Suzanna chose a blue, velvet dress that hung on her shoulders perfect and fell just below her knees. It showed her slim waistline and the color of the dress itself brought out the blue of her eyes. She completed it with her go to, single, pearl necklace and matching earrings. Simplicity was her middle name.

Steven couldn't keep his eyes off of her and Steven's mother noticed the look of love in her son's eyes. She was so happy for him to have found love a second time. Donna wore an elegant, black, flair leg, pant suit with a plunging neckline that showed off her ladies a bit more than Suzanna would, but hers were not that showy either.

One by one, they all showed up and it was a bit overwhelming to try and remember everyone. Cousins and their children and Donna's two younger girls flew in from California just in time to eat. Their flight was delayed. Donna did her best at introductions, but everyone was basically on their own. Sammie was even late because of her shift at the hospital. Sammie is Donna's oldest daughter. She was lucky to have gotten off in time. A friend with no children offered to fill in for her at the hospital.

"Hi, Sammie, Merry Christmas!" Suzanna said. "Good to see you. I have been so busy since I've been here, we haven't seen each other much."

"I know, I'm sorry about that, but between the twins and the hospital I barely have time for myself anymore. I want to thank you for the money. Mom told me it came from you, and it was such a big help on getting settled and caught up on things. The hospital has daycare now, so it's so much better because I can take a long lunch and spend time with them and they love." Sammie said but I need to get over more. I know mom misses them" Sammie told her.

"No thanks needed, but your welcome," Suzanna said. "If you need anything, just holler. And I mean that."

"I really appreciate that," Sammie replied.

Donna walked up and gave her a hug. "Hi Mom, love you and Merry Christmas," Sammie told her mom with a big smile and a hug.

Donna got everyone rounded up to eat and instructed people to sit wherever they liked. There were just enough chairs, Praise God, Donna thought to herself.

Cousins reminisced as they ate and laughed about childhood antics while the children wanted to know why they couldn't do things like that. "Because you never get your nose out of your iPad," Ronald said to his son. "Not to mention getting you guys to play outside is harder than pulling teeth."

Donna agreed.

Everyone had a good time and plenty to eat.

"Compliments to the chef," Ronald offered. They all cheered.

"I had plenty of help," Donna said, "but thanks for coming. Now if the adults want to go upstairs, we are playing a little soft Christmas music if anyone wants to dance."

Deb went over to Suzanna and told her she was going to stay downstairs with the kids. If Mandy got tired, she would go on to bed. "I figure you are going to Steven's tonight, right?"

"Okay, Sis, are you okay?" Suzanna asked.

"Oh yes, just a wee bit tired myself. Being a new mommy is a bit demanding, but I love it and would have it no other way," Deb answered.

"By the way, you look beautiful tonight in your emerald, green, satin dress and Mandy was so adorable in that long pink princess dress," Suzanna added. "If nobody knew the difference, they would believe she was your natural born child. I am so happy for you, Sis. Is everything okay? Any hiccups or anything you are concerned about?"

"No, not really," Deb answered. "Mandy is making a good transition. If anything, maybe too good. I want to make sure she feels comfortable talking to me about anything. I do have a children's therapist set up for her to see two weeks after we get back to Kentucky. I have taken her shopping for some new clothes, some bedroom blankets and pillows, and other things. I just expected her to talk about her mom a bit more and it's been crickets.

Chapter 40

Thanks for asking, Sis. You could always read my moods. I have contemplated moving here if that would help her adjust, but she seems to be excited to be moving to Kentucky."

"Do you want Steven to have a little talk with her?" Suzanna asked.

"That might be a good idea. She loves and trusts him. It would at least alleviate some of my concerns. Thanks, Sis. I love you."

"Love you too Sis."

Chapter 41

After unwrapping presents, Stevens parents went to bed. His mother gave Suzanna a beautiful, heirloom, country star quilt. Suzanna absolutely loved it.

"I feel so bad I didn't make it to the candlelight service tonight, but I felt I needed to help Donna," Suzanna confessed to Steven. "Do you think your parents think poorly of me/ I promise, no matter what, I will never miss again."

"Honey, my parents are not judgmental like that. They understood, but most important I understand. I know you have a heart for God and that's all that matters to me." Steven assured her as he looked down into her eyes and she looked into his with so much love in her heart it hurt. They were wrapped up in the quilt Steven's mother gave her and they sat in front of the fireplace. "I have another present for you.," Suzanna said. She pulled out a small, green, satin, jewelry box from under the couch where she hid it earlier. She handed it to him.

"What's this?" Steven asked. He took it from her, still looking into her eyes.

"Go ahead, open it," she prompted.

He opened the box to find an Irish *claddagh* ring. It had blue, green, and red stones all around it. "This has to be a very expensive ring," Steven said. "It is exquisite."

"It was in with the stuff my brother found with the will and other things. Those stones are genuine diamonds colored somehow the Irish did things

Chapter 41

but I took it to the jewelers after we sized our wedding bands and had it sized and cleaned and found it is a very, very expensive ring."

He looked at her as she placed it on his right hand. He smiled at her. "How very, very?"

"Oh, very, very, very, very expensive." She laughed.

He looked at the ring and then at her and reached under her arms and tickled her and turned her over and laid her gently across the couch and came down to kiss her. She was still laughing when his lips touched hers. For a moment, they were one as his kiss turned so passionate she didn't want to wait another minute— much less another week—to be all his. The heat between them grew even more the longer his lips lingered on hers, gently nibbling on the both the top and the bottom of her soft, moist lips. Then he turned to her neck, the spot that always sent chills down her spine, and warmed her insides to boiling.

The guest bedroom door opened. "Do you have something for acid indigestion?" Julie asked. "Your father ate too much turkey. He knows better than to eat too much turkey, but he just couldn't resist the temptation."

She walked into the room just as Suzanna straightened her hair and sat up.

"Suzanna fell asleep under your beautiful quilt Mom," Steven said. "Just a minute. I think I have something for him."

His Mother looked at the two of them for a long minute. She trusted her son to be admirable, but she knew during a weak moment that things could get out of control.

"Perhaps you both should call it a night and get some real rest," she said innocently and respectfully. "Tomorrow will be another busy day and the week is going to get even more hectic. Come on sweetheart, let me help you get settled and Steven you are sleeping in your study aren't you sweetheart."

"Yes Mom. But if you or Dad need anything, don't worry about waking me. I'm a light sleeper," Steven said.

"Goodnight, dear," she said.

"Goodnight, Mom," Steven answered. He gave her a peck on the cheek and handed her the acid indigestion medicine for his dad.

Suzanna allowed her to walk her into Steven's bedroom, which was already fixed for her to spend the night. She felt like a young schoolgirl being chastised by her mom. Thanks, Julie."

"Sweetie, I was young once and I do remember how temptation can get to the best of us. I also know you and Steven would be so full of guilt if you became intimate just a week before your wedding and it could allow feelings of guilt to fester. That's how Satan tries to destroy the sanctity of marriage. I didn't mean any disrespect. I'm just trying to protect both of you and what you have is so special, I don't want anything to get in the way of your happiness and fulfillment."

"I totally understand and respect that." Suzanna turned and gave her a big hug. "I love you Mom, good night."

Julie winked. "I love you too kiddo, goodnight."

Chapter 42

After lunch on Christmas Day, Bill and Julie headed back to Lincoln. They wanted to get ahead of some wintery weather they had predicted for later in the day. Steven and Suzanna headed to Donna and Richard's house. There would probably a long Monopoly game in their future. They laughed just mentioning it.

Sure enough, turkey sandwiches, pumpkin pie and Monopoly war. Even Abigail was over to play a game of Monopoly. Steven promised Suzanna he would win because he learned Mike's strategy. Donna, Deb, and Suzanna were soon out of the game, accidentally on purpose and left it to the men to do their battles.

"Actually, I was too tired to give it too much of a try," Suzanna confessed. They were sitting on the big, comfy couch and Deb had the recliner. Mandy fell asleep in her arms, so she carried the girl downstairs for a nap.

"Julie got out of bed last night and caught Steven and me being intimate—almost too intimate if you know what I mean," Suzanna shared. With a laugh, she confessed how much she wanted to give herself to him. "I love him so much. It's so hard to hold back."

"But you both would regret it, and you know it," Donna cautioned her.

"One more week," Deb said.

"I know, I know but it is so hard." They all laughed at the choice of words.

"There is a lot to be said for waiting until you are married before God and man."

"I've had sex before," Deb confided. "I thought I loved him but all he wanted was a physical relationship. As soon as I actually said no, he left me."

"Sis, I'm so sorry. I never knew that. I should have been there for you. Was it Roger?" Suzanna asked.

Deb nodded and started to cry. "I hope I will someday have a Steven like you do."

Suzanna gave her a hug. "You will. You are beautiful and sweet, loving and caring, and smart. When the right person comes your way. God's perfect timing. Remember that."

"Everything is in God's time," Donna agreed. "Let's pray over her, Suzanna."

They both laid their hands on Deb's head and prayed for God to bring her a soul mate to love and who would love her and Mandy. They all three felt a chill as God's spirit moved. They all felt God had a plan. Deb just needed to remain faithful and believe.

"Sometimes we jump ahead of God when we get impatient in the waiting," Donna said.

"Trust me, she gives great advice," Suzanna added.

They all laughed through sad and happy tears. Through the joy of just knowing God and how He can be trusted with our life, through the beginning to the end.

Steven noticed they were praying and asked if there was anything he could do. They laughed.

"I think we've got it," Donna said. Steven looked puzzled, then he glanced at Suzanna and gave a smile, which she reciprocated.

Steven won the Monopoly game. Mike was crushed. Richard was shocked. The women didn't care; they were just ready for some hot chocolate. They all began discussing the wedding and what was left to get done.

"Andrea really has things under control as far as the reception goes," Donna said. "She has ordered all the flowers and the cake is under control. Andrea has three different menu ideas to run past you whenever you want to get to the store."

"Sure, we can go tomorrow if you guys want to. Do you think Mandy might want to be a flower girl?" Suzanna offered.

Chapter 42

Deb smiled. "I think she would love it. That would be awesome. I know at one point it was discussed but never mentioned again."

"You just pick out whatever you and her like and I'll pay for it. I trust your judgement. You know what everyone else is wearing so just take her shopping and have fun," said.

"Does that mean?" Deb started.

"Yes, just go crazy—the both of you—and buy whatever you need or want forever you need or want. You won't be here after this week, so indulge me and have a good time with her."

Suzanna and Deb stood up and hugged for a long time. "I'm going to miss you so much." Suzanna confessed. "You know they have schoolteachers here, too. Plus, handsome men and several at church are unattached."

"I've had my eyes open." Deb laughed. "For both actually."

Suzanna looked at her. "Really? For both? Any bites on either?" Suzanna joked back.

"Actually, yes," Deb said. "But nothing is concrete. Will have to wait until the New Year due to budget issues."

"My Sis, you have surprised me. I had no idea you were thinking about this, but it makes me so happy."

"You are the one who put the bug in my ear," Deb replied, "and I have grown to like it here. It feels so lonely the thought of going home. And leaving you here permanently."

"I know, it's surreal to me as well." Suzanna admitted. "Whatever you need, just ask and it's yours. I love you, Sis."

Chapter 43

New Year's Eve

Suzanna, Deb, and Donna were a bundle of nerves. Everyone tried to stay calm for Suzanna, but they had their own problems. Their Nerves! The church was beautiful. Andrea outdid herself, but she was told the budget was limitless, so she held them too it. Though she was frugal in her spending and how she spent, she still did a topnotch job. Little did they know being winter and the pandemic continuing to create issues, there was a supply shortage of flowers. Andrea pulled it all together using more than one florist.

After the rehearsal the night before, everyone knew what, where, and how. They all went to their favorite pizza parlor after. Brother Jacobs would officiate, so he would be there to preach for the next two Sundays. The church board approved the time off and his replacement. Steven's parents made it just in time for the rehearsal.

"Bill, will you walk me down the aisle?" Suzanna asked. "You won't have to say anything, and you'll just sit down with Julie when you're done."

"I would be honored to," he loudly replied. Gave her a big hug and a kiss on the cheek and sat down beside his beautiful wife Julie.

Suzanna wasn't sure about the way they fixed her hair. They had it piled on top of her head with curly tendrils hanging all over. The veil wrapped around the bun on top of her head. And of course, the tiara. She always wanted to be a princess and she felt like one. Her dress flowed out perfect with the other slip they purchased. She liked her make up. Subtle but perfect

Chapter 43

for her complexion. Her bouquet was a beautiful bunch of red and white roses, and she had a couple of white lilies that hung down just a little and tied with ribbon and lace.

Suzanna turned to look at Deb, Donna, and little Mandy holding on tightly to her flower girl basket with red and white rose petals inside.

"You guy look amazing." Suzanna tried to keep from crying to avoid messing up her makeup.

They all reached for each other and formed a tight circle, holding hands.

"You, my dear, are the most beautiful bride I have ever seen," Donna said to Suzanna. "You are breathtaking. You are stunning. You are beautiful."

"Enough with the flattery, she will get a big head," Deb said. "You do look amazing though. Steven is so lucky to have you."

"We are blessed to have each other," Suzanna corrected.

"You are very pretty Aunt Suzanna," Mandy said.

Suzanna bent down and smiled. "Thank you, Mandy. I think you are the prettiest flower girl I have ever seen."

"Me too," Mandy said. She looked down at her long white dress—she looked like a bride. The three ladies looked at each other and laughed. Then Donna grabbed Suzanna and Deb's hands. "Let's pray a prayer of blessing before we go down. It's time, Suzanna. Are you ready?"

They held hands, including Mandy.

After a short prayer Suzanna said, "I have never been more ready."

With a drop or two of tears from the women, they walked out of their dressing room and got into position. The church was packed because the wedding was open to the entire congregation. The reception, however, would only have two hundred people.

The *Wedding March* began and the girls walked down first then Mandy who was a perfect flower girl and at the end of the isle she just threw all the rest of the roses up in the air and everyone laughed while she just grinned. And sat down beside Steven's Mother.

Everyone stood as a friend from church sung *Because You Love Me*. Then the bride walked down the aisle with Bill. At the end of the aisle, he gave her a kiss on the cheek and sat down beside Mandy.

Suzanna took her spot beside Deb and turned to face Steven, Richard, and Mike. They all looked so handsome. Brother Jacobs was handsome too, which did not go unnoticed by Deb. She took a great deal of noticing.

Brother Jacobs spoke on marriage and God, then he asked Steven and Suzanna the standard marriage questions.

"I understand you both have written your own vows," Brother Jacob said.

"Yes," Suzanna and Steven agreed. "We have."

Brother Jacobs asked Suzanna to speak first. Suzanna was a bit choked up at first, but Steven reached out and held both her hands in his. He whispered "it's okay I'm right here."

She smiled and shed a tear. He wiped it with his finger, and she found her voice.

"When I came here on business and to reconnect with family, I never dreamed God would lead me to something more precious than gold. It was like the minute our eyes met; I saw something I had never seen in another man. With you, I have always felt cherished. You have always made me feel safe, and secure, and loved. As God's word describes a marriage bond between a man and woman, I found that in you. I have felt from the beginning that with the two of us and God, we could accomplish just about anything. I will follow you to the moon and back. I have come home, my childhood home and it's so much more than that. Home is not a place; my home is in you. I promise that in sickness and in health, richer or poorer, I will be faithful and honor you because you are my true soulmate. When you hurt, I hurt. When you rejoice, I rejoice. I will love you forever and a day, and longer if God allows."

"Are you Ready Steven?" Brother Jacobs asked.

Steven looked at Jacob as a good and longtime friend, and he nodded his head as tears fell from His face.

"When my wife died three years ago, I never expected to marry again. I never expected to fall in love again. And then you walked into my life like a thunderbolt. Everyone kept telling me I needed to get myself back out there but I felt when it was time God would let me know. I knew the minute our eyes met that you would be the one to reopen my heart. I promise to love,

CHAPTER 43

adore, and cherish you the rest of my life. In sickness and in health, richer or poorer, I love you and will forever treat you like my princess. I promise to see you as God sees you—as His masterpiece—that He loves, listens too, and accepts with flaws and perfection you will always be my lasting love of my heart."

"Are you ready to exchange rings?" Brother Jacobs asked.

They both nodded. As they exchanged their wedding rings, together they recited, "With this ring, I thee wed."

They then stepped down and bent their knees to rest on a pillow. Suzanna got some help from Deb and Donna who straightened out a very full wedding gown.

Suzanna and Steven held hands and, there before all, they each said a private prayer to God. Most couldn't hear them. Some could, but the one it was intended to hear, had heard and that was God. When they finished their first personal prayer as husband and wife, they stood holding hands and faced each other. Father Jacobs introduced them as husband and wife.

They kissed and looked at one another and kissed again before they walked down the aisle to greet their friends and family. Deb, Donna, and crew left for the reception to help Andrea with anything she might need them to do while Steven and Suzanna stayed behind to get some pictures.

To Suzanna's surprise, a white horse and white carriage were waiting to take them to the reception at their home. A large group was outside to greet them with cheers and bird seed. It was a beautiful, sunny, warm day for New Year's Eve in Omaha, Nebraska, but there was about seven inches of snow on the ground from two days prior.

People went through a buffet line and were served their choice of a Cornish hen or prime rib and all the extras, which began with a self-serve salad bar. Greeters wearing name tags showed them where to sit.

Closer friends got a quick walk through of the house. When Suzanna and Steven entered the house, they were amazed at how beautiful and festive Andrea had made their home with the red and white roses as the central theme of flowers she enhanced with so much more and lots of baby's breathe, lily's and so much more. The dining room and sunroom were combined to seat everyone. The enclosed indoor pool had been covered and would be used as a dance floor.

Soft music played while they ate. Deb, Mandy, Mike, Richard, and Donna sat with Steven and Suzanna. Everyone was so festive, happy, and full of laughter and congratulations. A table by the dance floor overflowed with more gifts than it could hold.

"I'm not a bit hungry," Suzanna whispered in Steven's ear.

"Neither am I," Steven confessed. "All I can think about is getting everyone to leave, so I can indulge in my marital rights."

Suzanna looked at him. "Me too."

They both laughed until Steven filled his mouth with hers to quiet their laughter. But it only made their desire grow for one another. They were so tired they would almost laugh at anything. Since the wedding reception was at their new home, Andrea took the precaution of having extra security dressed as ushers throughout the house and around the private areas of their home.

Steven and Suzanna melded into each other's arms as had their first dance. Bill filled in for Suzanna on the father and daughter dance. She cried throughout the dance and gave him a big hug when he kissed her on the cheek and told her that she was indeed his daughter now and it didn't matter what she needed, she could go to him.

At midnight, they all went outside to ring in the New Year with fireworks and cheer. Suzanna tossed her bouquet to the unmarried ladies, and Deb caught it. Deb and Brother Jacobs danced nearly every song together. Suzanna's little sister was smitten. Brother Jacobs seemed to enjoy himself well, too.

Deb, Mandy, Donna, Richard, and Mike stayed overnight in one of the spare bedrooms. After the reception, Andrea helped clean up. She hired caterers to do that, but she felt she needed to stay and oversee that everything was done properly.

"I wanted you to know you have done an amazing job," Suzanna said to Andrea. "And you can expect a sizable tip in the mail."

Chapter 43

"Oh Suzanna, thank you, but that's not necessary," Andrea said. "I am just thankful you gave me the opportunity to do this. You don't know what this has done for my business, and that's all the thanks I need."

"Well, let's just say that this will be just for you," Suzanna told her. "I really want to do this for you and if there ever comes a time you need anything just let me know. If it's possible, I will always be willing to help a friend."

"It has been such a pleasure doing this. It's been fun."

They hugged then Suzanna went to find her husband. He was in the living room with Donna and Richard. Mike, Deb, and Mandy had gone on to bed.

She walked into the living room and she could tell everyone was tired. She sat down beside Steven, and they gave each other a peck on the lips.

"Ready to go to bed sweetheart?" Suzanna asked.

"I've been ready for a few weeks." He joked.

She teasingly punched him lightly on the shoulder.

"Do you need any help getting out of your dress?" Donna asked innocently.

Suzanna looked at Donna then realized she had a hundred little buttons down the back of her dress.

"I think I can handle it," Steven said.

Suzanna started to protest then Steven put his index finger to her lips.

"I can handle it."

And down the hall toward the back of the house they walked hand in hand the way they will walk together the rest of their lives Donna thought. She turned to Richard to see if he was ready to go to bed. He had his head on one of the dozen pillows laying around. He was sound asleep and snoring. Donna looked at him for a minute. Bill and Julie walked past to go to bed. "

Honey, I have something that will fix that if you need something later," Julie said. "Just come and look us up." They walked down the hall hand in hand.

How sweet, Donna thought. She covered her husband up with one of the many blankets tossed around and then she curled up beside him with a soft fluffy blanket. She was asleep as her head hit the pillow on the other end of the couch.

Andrea walked by tying up loose ends and saw them asleep. She pulled out her iPhone and snapped a few pictures with a smile. She turned out the lights before she walked out the door and locked everything up. All her people were gone. When she turned around, she found the horse and buggy unattended in front of the house. She was at a loss for what to do. She didn't order a horse and buggy. Steven did that to surprise Suzanna. So, should she remind someone. As she stood there, the driver of the carriage came around the corner.

"Sorry, I had to go to the bathroom. Do you need a ride?"

"No, no I just didn't expect you to still be here. I sent all my people to go home," Andrea replied.

"Well, I guess I'll head out too then if they are not going anywhere tonight," said the driver.

"No, they are staying here tonight."

"You sure you don't need a ride?"

"I'm sure" she laughed. She climbed into her white, Dodge Ram with a trailer attached that was full of supplies she procured for the event. She was so thrilled that she was able to have had the opportunity to do that for such sweet people.

"Wow, I'm tired."

The horse and buggy had already left. She passed them on the road and waved.

Chapter 44

Steven and Suzanna reached their fresh, newly decorated bedroom. Andrea had placed a gift basket, flower petals on the bed, and chocolates on their pillows just as if they were in a fancy hotel.

"How sweet of Andrea to think of this." Suzanna commented as her husband began to unbutton all those tiny buttons while trying to kiss her neck. He made great time as she slipped out of her dress. He grabbed her around the waist and kissed her hard on the lips. She pushed him back. "Slow down tiger, let me get my dress hung up and get refreshed."

He didn't say a word. He plopped down on the edge of the bed and impatiently waited while she spent what seemed like hours in the bathroom. She walked out of their bathroom with a beautiful, long, soft nightgown on. The sleeves hung on her shoulders and as she walked into the room, she found her love asleep on the bottom edge of the bed. She pulled down the covers and walked over to her husband, "Finally," she thought. She started to take his pants off and lay them on the floor. That didn't wake him, but when she unbuttoned his shirt and started kissing him on his lips, softly at first then a little stronger, he turned her over on the bed and they were finally husband and wife in the eyes of God.

Suzanna had chills go up her spine as she discovered her husband was an excellent lover, which was on top of every other perfect thing about him. They were so much in love, his tenderness and passion melded into one as his patience with his wife—a virgin—learned his ways and he learned hers. Two became one that night, and they both could not be any happier as they fell asleep in each other's arms. Their passion satiated and completed they slept like babies until they heard a knock on the door. Donna and company had sent Deb to wake the newlyweds.

"You guys need to get up and come eat the breakfast Andrea left us.," Deb said. They looked at each other and turned to the clock. Steven jumped up when he noticed the time. "Come on young lady, we need to get up so everyone can go home."

She turned around and gave him a kiss. He jumped up like an alarm fire bell rang.

"Okay, okay, but I am just going to throw my robe on."

She had a long, soft, white robe to go over her nightgown. They walked out hand in hand and went into the kitchen where they made them hot chocolate and coffee. Donuts, bagels, and warm cream cheese were waiting for them.

"Wow, Andrea's blessings just don't stop," Suzanna commented.

Everybody sat around and the house was actually back to normal. Steven's parents were even still there. "Did everyone get a goodnight's sleep?" Suzanna asked.

"Did you?" Donna asked.

Suzanna blushed. "Not as much as I'd have liked."

"Richard and I slept on your big, comfy couch. So, I really don't know about anyone else. Donna answered. "Well Steven, haven't you told her yet?"

"Haven't had the time." He confessed.

"Don't you think it may be time to tell her?" Donna responded.

"Tell me what? What's wrong, Steven?" she asked.

"Haven't you thought about a honeymoon?" Steven asked her.

She looked around the room at everyone's sheepish smiles.

"No not really. I knew you took a couple weeks off from preaching, but I just figured our new home was like a honeymoon. I never thought anything about a honeymoon. Steven, what's up?"

He took her hand, the one without the bagel in it, and told her, "I wanted to surprise you with a two-week trip to Ireland."

Chapter 44

Suzanna dropped her bagel and held his other hand as she looked around the room at all the smiles. "Are you serious? You guys are not joking?" They all shook their heads as she turned to Steven. She saw the loving yet I'm serious look on his face. She jumped into his arms and kissed his face all over.

"As long as you guys make it to the airport in an hour," Donna said.

"But I'm not packed. We're not packed." Suzanna began to panic.

"Yes, you are," Deb replied. "You have been my sister long enough; I knew exactly what you would take. And Steven packed his own bags days ago."

"So, get your buns up and get dressed," Julie said.

"We will take care of everything else." Donna assured her.

"Oh, my goodness," Steven gasped. Everyone turned to look at him. "I forgot all about the horse and buggy last night."

"Andrea told me this morning that she told him it was okay to go." Donna laughed. "He was out there when she left. He was waiting on you guys to leave. You are probably going to owe him more money for the over time because that was around five or after. "No worries," he said, "I married an heiress."

Everyone went to the airport to say goodbye. It was bittersweet that Deb and Mandy would head back to Kentucky before Suzanna got back. Then Deb mentioned that she and Father Jacob had a date planned. "Who knows Sis, you may have started something here."

"Thank you guys, for everything," Suzanna told everyone, and hugs were passed all around. As they headed beyond where any visitors were allowed. They held hands tightly until they were seated on the plane. Once seated, it wasn't long before they took off. They relaxed in their seats and smiled at each other.

"Thank you for this," Suzanna said. "It was a complete surprise. I never even gave a honeymoon a thought. Do we have an itinerary and reservations and everything?"

"We do," Steven replied. "One thing, my friend has found some clues about your grandfather. I'm hoping to get more information about him after we land in Dublin. We will stay a couple days there doing a little research and sight-seeing before we start to adventure beyond.

He continued to mesmerize her as he told her some of the things he planned. "There is an eight-hundred-year-old pub that John F. Kennedy visited in 1965, I want to visit the Doolin Cave. You must go down 210 steps, which is 210 feet down to even enter the main part of the cave. I want to visit Doolin Music Capital of Ireland and visit The Burren National Park. There is the Blarney Castle where we have to be held upside down to kiss the Blarney stone. They have a poison garden there. I thought you would like to visit The Waterford Crystal Co., The River Liffey, and the abandoned ruins of the potato famine from 1840. I want us to visit the ten most beautiful church's in Ireland and the ten best castles, for which we will stay in a couple of them overnight." He looked at her and gave her a peck with a huge grin on his face.

She picked up a small pillow. "You are just reciting me trivia you learned while planning the trip. She turned an eye toward the man she had learned to love with all his excitement. She was tired. "Aren't you dear?"

He smiled as he pulled out his pillow. "I am."

Suzanna grinned and thought that life would be an amazing adventure with her man.

"Just one question sweetheart."

"Anything, honey," he answered.

She looked into his beautiful, intense eyes and asked as seriously as she could. "Why didn't you use my credit card and get first class seats?"

She smiled at him before she put an eye mask over her eyes, so she could take a long nap.